THE GOVERNESS GAMBIT

ERICA RIDLEY

THE GOVERNESS GAMBIT

A WILD WYNCHESTERS PREQUEL

CHAPTER 1

June 1816
Palace of Westminster
London, England

*M*iss Chloe Wynchester sucked in one last breath of semi-clean air from the open attic windows and then poked her head through one of the narrow apertures high above the central chandelier in the House of Commons.

Her nostrils immediately tickled with the smoke from dozens of flickering candles and the musty scent wafting from a large chamber packed with several hundred men.

The octagonal ventilation shaft was her only viewing gallery. Women had no place in Parliament. But Chloe never allowed anything so dull as *not belonging* to keep her from somewhere she wished to be.

Much of this blessing was due to her eminently forgettable nature. She was neither tall nor short, thin nor fat, ugly nor beautiful. Her clothes were neither fashionable nor tattered, her hair neither smartly curled nor a mess of tangles. Her eyes and hair were brown, the most common color. Her skin was white, neither pockmarked nor freckled. Having one of those faces that was always vaguely familiar was brilliant for pretending to be an old acquaintance.

Chloe was not a lady. She was a Whitechapel foundling, now grown to almost eight and twenty years. She'd had the immense fortune to be plucked from the orphanage and fostered by a foreign lord at the age of ten, but most orphans were not so lucky.

That was why she was here.

Chloe never missed a session of Parliament if she could help it, in order to stay abreast of any news of the government doing something—*anything*—to help the poor.

Most often, when the subject of money arose, the government's aim was to put coin in their pockets, rather than give aid to those who had none.

Parishes had workhouses, did they not?

There were foundling hospitals for orphaned infants, were there not?

The sort of thing a wealthy man might say, because he'd never been abandoned in a wicker basket, or had to wonder if tomorrow there might be a crust of bread to eat, or collapsed from exhaustion after working from dawn to dusk for months on end without a single day's respite.

It wasn't that the members of Parliament didn't *know* this was happening.

They didn't care enough to do something about it.

It was not their business.

This was just how the world worked.

None of which stopped Chloe from penning and disseminating countless pamphlets in an attempt to educate the wealthy on the plight of poverty. There were a few ladies' societies dedicated to charity for the poor, and Chloe appreciated them very much. Women like that were the reason she'd had somewhere to *go* as a newborn squalling inside of a basket.

But for big improvements, structural improvements, *lasting* improvements, one was forced to rely on the opinions of a chamber full of rich white men in top hats and tailcoats slowly sweating themselves into a puddle. They sat hip-to-hip with each other on long, narrow benches as the summer sun beat down upon the roof.

She pulled her head out of the ventilation shaft for another gulp of marginally-less-fusty air before returning her face to the smoky draft inside.

There he was.

Her heart beat faster.

The statesman with the rich, smooth voice was the reason she had hope.

Lawrence Gosling, Marquess of Lanbrooke, was the orator Chloe most loved to watch. It was not because of his soft brown hair or angular jaw. Or his wide shoulders displayed to perfection in a bespoke gray coat, paired with sharp black breeches over strong, muscular legs.

It was because Lanbrooke sometimes spoke about helping people who could not speak for themselves in Parliament.

Despite having to hunch over at an awkward angle to achieve a partially obstructed view, Chloe would not move from this position until Lanbrooke concluded his speech.

When he spoke, people listened.

She included the occasional pithy quote from him in her pamphlets, which made the content seem less idealistic and more official. If the future Duke of Faircliffe agreed with certain points, the public might think, surely some of the other ideas also had merit.

Eventually, when Lanbrooke inherited the Faircliffe dukedom, he would take his seat in the House of Lords. Although there was no convenient attic theatre box above that chamber, Chloe had no doubt Lanbrooke would continue to champion unpopular causes there just as often as he did here in the House of Commons. After all, she'd been watching him speak for almost a decade.

In fact—

A rhythmic knocking sound came from the roof just overhead.

Tat, rat-a-tat, tat.

It was the signal.

With one last look at her favorite statesman, Chloe eased her head out of the small square hole she'd been peeking through and blinked around the attic.

Occasionally the wife of a Member of Parliament would come to watch part of the proceedings, or the housekeeper—whose private chamber was up here in the attic—might pass by with a broom and a dustpan.

Today, Chloe was alone.

Not that it mattered. No one would remember her presence anyway. Chloe's relentlessly ordinary features were bland enough not to be describable in any identifiable way.

Over the years, she'd cultivated her forget-tableness by never meeting eyes or making conversation unless absolutely necessary, and even then ensuring each encounter was as ordinary and unremarkable as possible. This skill had allowed her to slip past countless witnesses, without leaving any clear memory of the meeting behind.

Tat, rat-a-tat, tat.

"Yes, yes," she muttered under her breath. "I heard you the first time."

There must be an adventure afoot.

She strode to an open window and made the answering knock on the wooden frame so that her brother Graham would know his message had been received and heeded.

Her brother had never met a structure he couldn't easily scale. Graham needn't bother with anything so mundane as stairs. A flying buttress? No problem. He could sprint up it to the rooftop as nimbly as a squirrel.

Chloe, on the other hand, was obliged to take the stairs.

She hurried down, leather half-boots padding silently on the wooden steps, the handsome MP already forgotten. There were more important things than Parliament.

The Wynchester siblings didn't just *talk* about doing good works.

The Wynchester siblings *delivered*.

Whenever there was a problem the system couldn't—or wouldn't—attend to, Chloe and her tight-knit family of fellow orphans turned their unique talents to finding justice.

It was time for another mission.

CHAPTER 2

*C*hloe leapt from her carriage the moment it paused at the Wynchester family's large home in semi-fashionable Islington. She raced up the path to the entrance.

Their butler, Mr. Randall, had the door open long before Chloe reached it.

"Everyone is in the blue parlor," Mr. Randall said as he took her bonnet. "The poor woman is in quite a state. She won't speak to anyone but you."

"*Me?*" Chloe repeated in surprise.

The only people who ever remembered her lived under this roof: the various Wynchester siblings, their foster father Baron Vanderbean, known familiarly as Bean, and a household of cherished servants.

For someone else to remember her—to ask for her—to *need* her!

Chloe thanked Mr. Randall over her shoulder as she rushed to the blue parlor.

Bean was in his usual armchair, a gorgeous cream-and-red bergère. As usual, his snow-white hair was impeccably styled, and his quick blue eyes were the first to notice Chloe. Very little got past Bean. He was the one who had taught her that any good strategy began with keen observation.

To his left sat handsome, brown-skinned Jacob Wynchester, with a golden puppy on his lap. Jacob was usually out in the barn training or rescuing one animal or another, but he always joined the family whenever a client was in trouble. His dark eyes were on their guests.

Tommy Wynchester sat on his other side, her frock coat gorgeously tailored and her cravat impeccable. Only her short brown hair was tousled, as though she'd recently dragged her fingers through it.

Behind them, standing against the silk-covered walls, was golden-skinned, black-haired Graham Wynchester. He must have *flown* home from the Palace of Westminster to beat Chloe here and yet somehow, he managed to look refreshed and presentable.

Elizabeth Wynchester sat on one of the sofas, her hands folded on the serpentine handle of her cane, which concealed a sharp blade. Her chin rested atop her folded hands and her sharp green eyes glittered.

Next to her was diminutive Marjorie Wynchester, her face and fingers flecked with colored paints. She spent most of her time in her third-floor studio, creating works of art or forging someone else's.

On the opposite sofa was a distraught matron with a familiar face.

Mrs. Pine.

With apple cheeks and bright gray eyes framed with laugh lines, Mrs. Pine was usually a ray of sunshine in a dark place. She worked at the orphanage where Chloe had grown up. Mrs. Pine had been the one who discovered her basket on their front step and brought it in from the cold.

Mrs. Pine had known Tommy for just as long but could be forgiven for not recognizing her. The tall figure in trousers and a waistcoat did not resemble the little girl named Thomasina.

Tommy rarely left home as the same person twice, unless a mission required it. Some days she was a gentleman, others a lady. Sometimes old, sometimes young. It was impossible to fathom what mischief she'd been in the midst of when the knock came at the door.

Next to Mrs. Pine sat a young girl, anywhere between eight and twelve years of age. She looked healthy, but childhood malnourishment often made it difficult to determine age at a single glance. At least she was with Mrs. Pine now. The motherly woman would do everything in her power to keep the girl safe.

"You're here!" Mrs. Pine sprang up from the sofa and rushed to greet Chloe. "I knew you'd come to the orphanage soon—we are all forever indebted to your family for the quarterly donations—but I'm afraid this couldn't wait. I'm in... I have... a bit of a pickle."

"She has me," the skinny little girl on the couch said defiantly. "*Again.*"

"And with me you'll stay," Mrs. Pine assured the child. "That is, I hope so. I haven't any authority to... but that's why we're here. Chloe's family solves hopeless cases for the desperate. I never thought to become a hopeless case myself, but... Well, here we are. You're my last resort and my only hope. Please tell me you can help."

"We'll do our best," Bean promised. "No matter what it is. Please, take your seat and tell us about it. Leave nothing out."

Chloe settled into an empty armchair between Bean and Mrs. Pine.

"The problem is... Well, no, you're not a problem, darling, I don't mean it like that. I'm just trying to... This is Dot." Mrs. Pine placed her arm reassuringly about the child's shoulders. "She came to us as a foundling nine years ago. Last month, she was fostered by a wealthy family outside of Benson."

Chloe and her siblings exchanged raised eyebrows. A rich benefactor was an unlikely achievement for an orphan. Finding Bean was the single greatest thing that had happened to them. But despite this stroke of good fortune, something must be gravely wrong.

"Being placed with a family of means is lovely," Chloe said. "Congratulations."

Dot glared at her.

Mrs. Pine winced apologetically. "She sneaked back."

"Sneaked... *back?*" Chloe repeated.

Baron Vanderbean had been the best thing to happen in any of the Wynchester siblings' lives. They wouldn't *be* siblings if he hadn't found them and adopted them, giving them a name and a family and a purpose.

She knew from experience that a kindhearted philanthropist such as Bean was the exception to the rule, but Chloe also knew how it felt to try to fall asleep in a narrow lice-ridden cot whilst her stomach twisted painfully in hunger. She would have traded anything for a clean bed and a warm meal.

The orphanage was less dreadful now—due in no small part to the Wynchesters' gifts and donations—but all the same, it was an *orphanage.*

Something awful must have happened to make Dot run away from her new family.

She turned to Dot and spoke gently. "Tell me about it."

"They said they wanted me. They *didn't*." Dot crossed her arms and held Chloe's gaze despite the sudden glossy sheen reflecting in her eyes. "They tossed me away."

"To a boarding school," Mrs. Pine explained quickly. "Except it wasn't. I'm getting ahead of myself."

"It's all right," said Chloe. "Start at the beginning. We have as much time as you need."

Mrs. Pine nodded gratefully. "The family consisted of a mother, a father, and a daughter, who had begged endlessly for a sibling to play with. After years with no luck, they decided to foster an orphan about the same age as their daughter, in order to give her the playmate she'd always desired. Dot seemed perfect. Dot, you *are* perfect. Don't let small-minded people—"

Dot turned away with her nose in the air, blinking rapidly.

"The daughter decided she could not abide sharing her parents' attention after all," Mrs. Pine said with a sigh. "The parents were too well bred to give a child they'd promised to raise *back* to the orphanage she'd come from. They felt an obligation to see to Dot's future, and meant to make good on it. So they sent her to boarding school."

"It is not a school," Dot said darkly. "It's a workhouse."

Mrs. Pine let out a sigh. "It was for you, and for that I am sorry." She turned back to Chloe. "Sarah Spranklin's Seminary for Girls is an institution just outside of London that accepts boarders year-round."

Dot hugged herself tight. "My 'family' didn't want me back."

"The school has a special program," Mrs. Pine explained. "At a discount in tuition, the child helps with chores and is later placed in gainful employment, such as that of governess, which is very respectable."

"It would be," Dot agreed. "If it happened."

Mrs. Pine's mouth tightened. "Dot says none of the girls in the 'special program' have any contact with the other students, other than to cook their meals, wash their clothes and dishes, and empty their chamber pots. They work all day, with little time to do more than sleep on hard pallets and begin the day all over again. Dot's tuition was paid in advance from now until she reaches her majority."

"I assume they couldn't contact their families," Bean said quietly.

Dot's lower lip wobbled. "We haven't pen or

paper, nor time to use them even if we did. Some who've lived there since they were small can scarcely read or write. We're kept in the attic, except when we're working. And always under Miss Spranklin's watchful eye."

"Heaven forgive me, I thought Miss Spranklin was *nice*." Mrs. Pine's voice cracked. "She visited the orphanage last year, and ended up taking a young girl named Agnes home with her. I thought... I thought it was a fairytale. Like Chloe and Thomasina, Agnes was kind and clever. I thought she'd make a brilliant governess."

"Agnes makes porridge and boiled vegetables," Dot said. "She's in the kitchen before dawn and cannot sleep until the last dish is clean."

"*I* put her there," Mrs. Pine whispered, her face pale and her eyes tortured. "I signed the papers and let her go with nothing more than a smile and a wave."

"You didn't know," Chloe said softly. "From the sound of it, no one knows but Miss Spranklin and the girls themselves."

She could still remember the wretched indecision she'd felt when Bean had offered to give her a home. He was rich and titled. Even at ten years old, it had sounded too good to be true. The only adult who had ever treated Chloe with compassion was Mrs. Pine. It was thanks to her encouragement that Tommy and Chloe were now safe and comfortable and part of a big, loving family.

Bean's forehead lined. "Perhaps this 'school' is a ruse that allows Miss Spranklin to collect money as well as unpaid servants. Particularly if she specializes in 'teaching' children who aren't expected to ever return home."

Mrs. Pine twisted her hands. "Dot's foster family must have thought they were providing for her. They could rest easy, confident they'd left her better off than how she'd started."

"I'd rather live in the orphanage with you than go back to Miss Spranklin," Dot said.

Mrs. Pine took the girl's hand and squeezed. "You and Agnes were my favorites and I could scarcely bear to part with you, but I thought... if you could have a home like Chloe and Thomasina had found... It had seemed like a miracle then, and I wanted you to have a miracle, too."

Chloe's heart twisted. She hated to think that her good fortune had led to Agnes and Dot's *mis*fortune. She wished every orphan could find a Bean. Instead, Dot and the other girls had been saddled with Miss Spranklin, who seemed to feel orphans were tools to be used, not children to be loved.

"You're not going back," Chloe assured Dot. "First thing in the morning, Baron Vanderbean can file charges of—" Absolutely nothing. Chloe winced. "I see your point. We have no legal standing. Miss Spranklin was *paid* to take custody of Dot."

Mrs. Pine nodded unhappily. "The courts can't help us. I went to Bow Street and pleaded with the magistrate, all to no avail. They'll do nothing without proof of wrongdoing, and I have no evidence that laws have been broken. Chores are legal. Boarding schools are legal. Workhouses are legal. I'm just an old fool. They told me not to bother them again."

"She said we'd go to gaol if we ran away." Dot's eyes were wide. "I did it anyway."

"You're not going to gaol." Mrs. Pine turned back to the Wynchesters and grimaced. "The contract I signed for Agnes was similar to an apprenticeship. It's legally binding."

"Dot is back in the orphanage?" Chloe asked.

"Not with the other children," Mrs. Pine answered. "She stays in my small office whilst I'm working, and then sleeps in my room with me. I know it's not ideal... If Miss Spranklin were to return, and happened to spy her..."

"Dot can stay with us," Chloe said without hesitation. She didn't need to ask Bean and her siblings to know they would happily open their home and their hearts. "We've plenty of guest rooms and—"

"*No.*" Dot threw her arms about Mrs. Pine and

burst into tears. "Please don't take me from her. Not again."

Chloe remembered all too well what it had felt like to leave Mrs. Pine, the closest thing to a mother figure Chloe had ever known. She could just imagine Dot's joy at being adopted by wealthy family, only to be abandoned all over again. This time, at an institution where there was no Mrs. Pine. Just grueling hours of drudgery and hopelessness.

"Of course." Chloe's voice scratched. "You're right. You should live wherever you choose."

Dot sobbed into Mrs. Pine's chest, inconsolable.

"Look." Jacob knelt before her with the puppy in his arms. "Would you like to pet Goldenrod whilst the rest of us form a plan?"

Dot peeked over her shoulder.

"I warn you," Elizabeth said from the sofa. "That puppy is a chatterbox and none of her jokes are funny."

Dot let go of Mrs. Pine. "Puppies can't talk."

"I can!" said the puppy.

Dot squeaked and fell back against the cushion in surprise.

"Won't you hold me?" asked the puppy.

Dot narrowed her eyes at Jacob with suspicion. "How are you doing that?"

"It was me." Elizabeth could throw her voice

and make it sound like anyone—or anything—she chose. She smiled at Dot.

The little girl reached out her arms. Jacob placed the puppy in her lap. She immediately licked Dot's cheek, to her surprise and delight.

The butler, Mr. Randall, appeared in the doorway. "Pardon the interruption—"

Before he could explain further, the interruption himself flew into the parlor with a framed painting beneath one arm.

The Duke of Faircliffe. *Father* to Chloe's favorite politician. A man who visited several times a year. Whenever he needed money.

Chloe stepped in his path. "Your Grace, this is not the moment for—"

The duke swept past her, heedless of his boots scraping mud against the hem of Chloe's dress. Commoners were no more important to him than dust motes.

"I'm in a bad way," the duke said to Bean. "You like unusual paintings. Why not purchase this one? *The Three Witches of* Macbeth. See the witches? It'll match the demon painting you bought last time. Isn't it nice?"

Chloe turned to Mrs. Pine. "I'm sorry. He'll leave in a moment."

"Perhaps he can help us," Mrs. Pine said, her eyes bright.

"I wish he would," Chloe murmured back.

"Unfortunately, he never helps anyone but himself. Without grounds for a legal case, even a peer is limited on what he can do."

"Then it's hopeless?" Mrs. Pine asked, her voice bleak.

"Nothing is hopeless," Chloe said firmly. "Lords may be powerless, but Wynchesters can do anything."

"I've two other canvases out in my curricle," the duke was saying to Bean. "If you'd rather purchase one without witches—"

"I'd rather not have you barging into my parlor while I'm entertaining guests," Bean replied evenly.

The duke's cheeks bloomed with color. "You cannot speak to me like that, you... you..." He seemed to remember where he was and why he was there. "It's worth five hundred pounds. I've had it appraised. You can have it for three hundred. Two hundred, if you must."

"I don't want it at all." Bean arched a brow. "As you mentioned, we've already got one."

Their painting was called *Robin Goodfellow in the Forest with Fairies*, but the Wynchesters called it *Puck & Family*, and considered it a family portrait.

In Shakespeare's *A Midsummer Night's Dream*, Puck was a mischievous imp who played tricks and meddled, often in an attempt to improve the lot of those around him. In the painting, Puck and six other merry goblins danced in a circle in a magical forest. Puck was Bean, and the sprites were the siblings.

The summer that Bean had assembled his motley group of orphans, the Duke of Faircliffe had come to the house in much the same state he was in now. Out of money, and hoping to sell items from his home to chase creditors away.

Puck & Family had been the Wynchesters' first acquisition as a team. For several of the children, it had been the first item they'd ever owned. They loved it because it symbolized their bond and their new future together as a family. The painting belonged to them, just like the Wynchesters belonged with each other.

The duke didn't understand any of that. According to the gossip columns Graham read, the duke barely spoke to his own son, and had sold almost every heirloom his family had ever had, only to return to the gaming tables the following night.

"One hundred and seventy-five pounds," the duke said desperately. "One hundred and fifty. Name your price."

"No, thank you," Bean lifted a palm. "If you'll excuse us, Your Grace?"

"One hundred pounds," said the duke. "That's my final offer."

"If we wanted more art in our parlor," said Elizabeth, "Marjorie could paint it. Or bring something home from all of those exhibitions she goes to." Elizabeth turned in her seat so that Marjorie could see her face. "Who will we see next Wednesday?"

"Albus Roth," Marjorie said loudly.

The duke tucked his painting back under his arm. "Albus Roth?"

"We're all curious," Chloe explained. "At the time Roth painted *Puck & Family*—I mean, *Robin Goodfellow*—he wasn't well known, but he's become popular in recent years, and is to have his first London exhibition next week."

"We should take *Puck & Family* with us," Jacob teased Marjorie. "Have it signed twice."

"Sell it to me," the duke demanded. "I want it back."

Every face in the parlor swung to him in disbelief.

"No," Bean said simply. "It belongs to us."

"Just because the artist wasn't famous *then*, but is becoming so *now*," Graham sputtered. "I suppose you think you can have it back at the same price you sold it, too!"

"Give it to me at once," the duke commanded imperiously. "I demand its return."

"Your Grace!" his driver called from out in the

corridor. "I see one of your creditors. We must flee!"

The duke dashed from the parlor.

Chloe raised an eyebrow at Elizabeth. "Didn't the duke say he drove himself here in a curricle?"

Elizabeth smiled innocently. "He'll remember that once he steps outside."

"It will be too late." Jacob grinned at his sisters. "Mr. Randall will bar the door tight behind him."

"I wish he wouldn't appear once a month with some canvas to sell, and then snub us on the streets as though *we* were the urchins," Graham grumbled.

"We *were* the urchins," Elizabeth reminded him. "There's no shame in being poor or an orphan."

"None at all," Chloe agreed, and turned back to Dot and Mrs. Pine. "You rescued one. We'll rescue the rest. We cannot leave children in such abominable conditions."

"We cannot rescue them *yet*." Graham rubbed his jaw. "If we go and kidnap a dozen young girls—"

"Two dozen," Dot murmured.

"—two dozen young girls," he amended, "people will notice and there will be questions. At the moment, Miss Spranklin has guardianship and the courts would side in her favor."

Chloe straightened. "If there is no law that can

stop her, then we have no choice but to shut down this so-called Seminary for Girls ourselves."

"I'll pay a visit tomorrow morning," said Bean. "Whilst Miss Spranklin is distracted with me, the rest of you can—"

Mrs. Pine shook her head. "I tried. No visitors allowed."

"Perhaps not from you or me," Chloe said gently. "But Bean is a *baron*—"

"Not even from lords." Mrs. Pine's expression was bleak. "Miss Spranklin allows no visits from anyone at any time of the year."

"Parents cannot see their own children?" Jacob said, appalled. "No holidays or outside contact of any kind?"

Mrs. Pine shook her head. "None at all. I suspect any parent that would agree to such terms must be like the family who abandoned Dot. Most children were placed there because they aren't wanted at home."

"Or don't have a home," Dot said. "Only a few students leave for Christmas or summer holiday."

"When is summer holiday?"

"The month of August," Dot answered. "Right after the musicale."

Mrs. Pine turned to stare at her. "The what?"

"The musicale," Dot repeated. "The girls whose parents do care enough to take them home for Yuletide expect their daughters to become respectable ladies. The annual musicale is when Miss Spranklin shows off how accomplished her students have become, and convinces the parents to pay higher tuition."

Chloe straightened. Perhaps that was their opportunity to search for evidence against Miss Spranklin. "There will be fewer people at the school for the entire month?"

Dot shook her head. "Not this time. Mrs. Spranklin is expanding the school. She hopes to house a dozen more students after the construction finishes."

"To finish in under a month, carpenters may have to work round the clock," Bean murmured.

Chloe nodded. They could not break in whilst the school was swarming with additional witnesses, nor could they wait for the carpenters to finish and risk a dozen more girls falling into Miss Spranklin's web. They had to act as swiftly as possible.

"We have one month," Bean said. "Let's not take more than a week."

CHAPTER 3

*E*arly the next evening, the Wynchester family reunited in the upstairs Planning Parlor, a sound-dampened private sitting room they used for plotting stratagems.

Chloe picked her way carefully across the dark slate floor, part of which already displayed a large chalk map of the Spranklin Seminary for Girls and its surroundings. Tommy was the one who scouted maps. Her careful disguises and casual demeanor let her stroll any street unchecked.

"Excellent work," Chloe said.

Tommy grinned back at her. "Thank you."

Bean and the siblings were scattered about the room in their usual spots. The Wynchester family had a habit of arranging themselves in the same order as the painting hanging above the mantel. The canvas bore their beloved forest scene of Puck and his happy, dancing imps. The idea of selling it back to the Duke of Faircliffe was laughable.

The painting was priceless.

Bean, being Puck, took the central winged chair with his back to the unlit fireplace. Although the beau monde considered him a recluse, the truth was Bean was frequently out in the world—just not in the sorts of places the aristocracy was likely to visit. He was the mastermind behind their missions.

Acrobatic Graham and easy-going Tommy sat in needlepoint armchairs between tall, open windows. A hint of gray had begun to cover the rich colors of sunset, and the scent of impending rain was thick in the air.

Lounging upon a chaise, delightfully bloodthirsty Elizabeth polished the serpent handle of her sword stick. Artistic Marjorie was lost in her own world, sketching at the long walnut-and-burl table with secret compartments in the center of the room. And strong, sensitive Jacob...

Chloe frowned. "Where's Jacob?"

"Out in the barn," Elizabeth replied.

"Jacob is training some animals he hopes might be useful on this mission," Tommy explained.

Graham closed his eyes. "Please tell me it's not weasels again. I can do without any more wild animals."

"They were useful," Tommy chided him. "They did exactly as Jacob trained them, and we were able to get justice for that nursemaid."

"Yes, but..." Graham shuddered. "*Weasels.*"

"Tommy, shall we begin with you?" Chloe prompted. "Tell us about the map."

Tommy raked her fingers through her short brown hair, leaving a streak of white chalk dust behind. She grabbed a long wooden rod to point out various aspects of the map.

"Elizabeth and I spent the day reconnoitering. That is the main road. This loop is just big enough for a dogcart, but it does circle around the school. These are walking paths, and *these*"— Tommy tapped with the rod—"could certainly be used to smuggle orphans out one by one."

"We cannot kidnap every child in the boarding school," Elizabeth reminded her.

"Of course we can," said Bean. "It's just not Plan Number One."

"Have we got a Plan Number One?" Graham asked.

"We're working on it," Elizabeth said. "Whilst Tommy was mapping escape routes from the grounds, I sneaked about counting windows and doors. If they had caught me doing so, I would have pretended I was on my way to visit a relative and had paused to rest beneath the shade of the school building. Once anyone sees my cane, they tend to assume I'm harmless."

Tommy grinned. "If only they knew the damage you can do with the hidden blade inside it."

"Only when my joints allow spry movement," Elizabeth said with a smile. On a good day, she could take down a pack of ruffians in seconds. "I counted twenty-five children, twenty of whom were in a salon being taught arithmetic. So there *is* education… for some of them."

"And the others?" Chloe asked in trepidation.

Elizabeth sighed. "The others were working their fingers to the bone, just as Dot described. It turns my stomach to report that the youngest of the lot appeared no older than six or seven years of age."

"It is one thing to offer gainful employment to an adolescent," said Graham. "It is quite another to exploit and terrify a child."

A maid and two footmen entered the room and laid the table for dinner.

"Thank you, Zinnia," Chloe said. "Please tell Mr. Randall that if a package arrives for me, he's to send it up at once."

"I suppose I know better than to ask what's in the package," Elizabeth murmured as she reached for a plate.

Chloe's cheeks flushed. She *did* receive a great

many packages, most of which were ushered straight into her private chamber, where they remained forever after.

"I have commissioned new calling cards," she explained. "You're looking at 'Jane Brown, Governess.'"

Tommy piled her plate with cakes. "I would have let you borrow one of my cards."

"I would make a terrible vicar or blacksmith," Chloe said with a grin. Tommy was the master of disguises, but Chloe rarely needed one at all.

"Jane Brown is looking for employment," Bean told Tommy. "Miss Spranklin may run her school by herself now, but when she expands, she will find herself in want of good help."

Chloe settled back in her chair. "Jane Brown is an experienced governess who has tired of her lot. She's considering teaching in a private school like the Spranklin Seminary for Girls, or failing that, providing administrative or secretarial assistance."

"Or failing that?" Graham asked. "No plan without a contingency."

"Failing *that*," Chloe said, "Jane Brown intends to open her own school. And who better to emulate than the enterprising businesswoman she most admires in all the world?"

"Ooh," Tommy said. "An appeal to Miss Spranklin's obviously considerable sense of superiority. She won't be able to brag about turning children into unpaid laborers under false pretenses, but she'll want to show off how clever she is."

"Since Miss Spranklin is looking to expand her school, she'll dislike the thought of competition," Bean said. "It would be better to have Jane Brown under her thumb than working against her."

Chloe nodded. "If she wishes to employ me, I'll begin at once. Perhaps imply with double the instructors, she could even raise prices."

"I wonder what she charges now," Elizabeth mused.

Graham pulled one of his handwritten albums from the low bookcase spanning the wall behind him and flipped through the pages.

"On 13 January of this year," he read aloud, "twenty private boarding schools published advertisements in the Oxford Journal. The Prospect House Boarding School run by the Misses Temple is listed at thirty-five guineas. The Spranklin Seminary for Girls is a comparatively affordable twenty-five."

"*Nothing* happens without Graham knowing about it," Elizabeth said with awe.

"And writing it down," Tommy added. "Or pasting it in."

Graham closed his album. "The most expensive and exclusive schools don't list their prices in the newspaper, because they've no need to advertise."

"Perhaps that is what she aspires to." Bean stirred sugar into his tea. "She must be an excellent saleswoman to charge as much as she does. She may see 'Jane Brown' as a wish come true."

"I'll do my best," Chloe said. "The role will put me in the perfect position for interior reconnaissance. If I see anything that can be used as evidence, I'll either make a note of it, or nick it outright."

"Good as done," Tommy said with a grin. "With Chloe's nimble fingers, she could smuggle children out using sleight-of-hand alone."

"We're not stealing them yet," Elizabeth said. "A house full of abducted children would be a complication. Their parents *paid* for them to be with Miss Spranklin."

"It's Plan Two," Bean agreed. "Shutting down her school is Plan Number One. All of the children will be much safer if the Spranklin Seminary for Girls no longer exists."

Tommy nodded and rose to her feet. "I'll see you all at dinner."

"It is not like Jacob to miss tea." Marjorie shook her head. "I wonder what animal he's training now."

"Shall we go and see?" Elizabeth suggested.

Graham looked horrified. "Absolutely not!"

"It might not be weasels," she protested. "It could be toads or cockerels."

"He has a Highland tiger," Graham reminded her as they exited the parlor. "Whatever the beast is, it's bound to be dangerous."

The footmen returned to clear the table, and then only Chloe and Bean remained.

She retrieved their respective novels from the bookcase and they settled into neighboring arm-chairs before the fireplace, as was their custom. Being summertime, there was no fire dancing in the grate, but that did not dampen the bliss she felt during the many calm hours she spent reading side-by-side with Bean.

Often, they traded novels after they finished, and then argued passionately over whether this character should have done that, or if this plot element would have been better served like that.

There was nothing Chloe cherished more.

"I wish I were your real daughter," she murmured without looking at him.

It was not the first time she'd voiced such a sentiment. Ever since she first met Bean eighteen years ago, she'd wished they'd always been to-gether from the beginning.

"You *are* my real daughter," Bean said gruffly. "Whenever you worry, just look at our portrait. See that?" He pointed at the painting above the mantel. "It's all of us. We *are* a real family. Never let anyone suggest otherwise."

Chloe gazed up at *Puck & Family* and a familiar sense of happiness and warmth settled over her.

"You're right," she said. "Family isn't blood, but rather our hearts. And no one's hearts are bigger than the Wynchesters.'"

Bean's smile was strained as he rubbed his temples.

She frowned and touched his shoulder. "What's wrong?"

"Just a megrim," he said. "It started a day or two ago."

"A day or two?" she repeated in alarm. Chloe placed the back of her hand against his forehead. "You're warm. You should lie down."

"I'm fine. Shall we read?" Bean plucked his novel from her grip and opened to the bookmark.

Chloe gazed at him for a long moment. "Are you certain you—"

"Here!" The Duke of Faircliffe burst into the parlor bearing a large vase in his hands.

"For the love of..." Bean put down his book and stood up. "Where is Mr. Randall?"

"I informed your butler that you were expecting a delivery."

Chloe had told Mr. Randall the same thing.

She covered her face with her hand. "*Calling cards.* I should have specified calling cards."

The duke acted as though he didn't even see her.

Perhaps he didn't.

She rose to block him from entering the room further.

The duke stepped around her without slowing.

"You were right," he said to Bean. "I cannot afford to purchase my painting back at any price. I haven't the blunt."

"*My* painting," Bean corrected. "It belongs to my family."

"Loan it to me," the duke begged. "Just for tonight. I'll bring it back in the morning."

Chloe narrowed her eyes.

Whatever the duke was planning, it certainly wasn't *that.* More likely, the inveterate gamester had wagered the painting away at a whist table before he'd remembered it was no longer in his possession.

That was too bad for him. *Puck & Family* would never leave the Planning Parlor. The duke would have to seek another method to make good on his debts. Only a fool would wager with him at this point. The duke was a wastrel and a gamester, and every morning the scandal columns mentioned his name.

It was a marvel his son had turned out so magnificently.

According to Graham, the duke's heir had never once been tempted by a gaming table. Against all odds, the handsome statesman was honorable, respectable, and *not kneeling on top of Tommy's map* with a cherub-shaped vase clutched in his hands.

"This is the most precious thing I own," the duke was saying to Bean. "I'll leave it in your custody as collateral security. I'll return to trade back in the morning."

Bean didn't even look at the vase. "No."

"I am sincere," said the duke. "Trust me, the last thing I want—"

A clatter sounded outside the open window, followed by flapping wings and the howl of an animal and breaking glass.

Chloe and Bean exchanged a startled glance. "*Jacob.*"

"We'll discuss this when I return," Bean told the duke.

Chloe was already racing down the rear stairs to the servants' entrance closest to the barn.

"Take the duke into the blue parlor," she heard Bean tell one of the footmen. "Keep him there."

Thunder sounded overhead. The first drops of cold rain spit down from the rapidly darkening sky.

Chloe raced across the lawn.

The door to the barn flung open and Jacob staggered outside. He shut the wide wooden door behind him and sagged against it. Rain streaked down his face and created new rivulets of red on his clothing. His shirt and trousers were ripped by claws. Stray bits of feather stuck to patches of blood all over his arms and chest.

"I'm fine," Jacob said. "It's nothing."

"You're covered in blood," Bean pointed out wryly.

"And claw marks," Chloe added. "Was it the tiger?"

"It was squirrels," Jacob said. "And a wild hawk. I made a slight miscalculation. Don't worry, everything will be ready when we need it."

"I can see that," Chloe said dryly. "Come inside. Let me help clean your wounds."

The crunch of carriage wheels on gravel came from the opposite side of the house, barely audible above the sound of driving rain.

"Thank God the duke left," she muttered. "I thought he would *never*—"

Her terrified gaze snapped to Bean's.

At once, he raced across the garden to the servants' entrance, nearly slipping and falling on the wet grass. Chloe frowned. Bean was usually agile. He must be as worried as Chloe was.

"What is it?" Jacob asked. "What's happening?"

"It had better be nothing," Chloe said darkly.

A poor choice of words, as it turned out. When they reached the Planning Parlor, a vase stood on the center of the marble mantel. And there on the wall, where the Wynchesters' cherished portrait had hung for eighteen happy years...

Was nothing at all.

CHAPTER 4

*C*hloe stalked into the breakfast room and slumped into her seat between her siblings.

It wasn't the footman's fault the Duke of Faircliffe had run out of the door with the family painting the day before. Servants could hardly be expected to tackle a peer of the realm. Especially not one as petty and single-minded as the duke. His first stop would have been to the magistrate to claim mistreatment.

"I'm sorry," Chloe said again. "I should have stayed behind to guard our portrait."

"No," Bean corrected. "I left him, too. You did the right thing. Family comes first."

"That *painting* is practically family." Her voice came out miserable.

"And we shall retrieve it," he said firmly.

"I cannot believe a duke stole from us," Elizabeth said.

"Faircliffe is more wastrel than duke," Graham reminded her. "He hasn't taken his seat in the House of Lords in years."

"Not even to vote on his son's bills," Chloe added. The duke had mastered the art of caring only for himself.

"Albus Roth is a famous artist now," Marjorie added. "The duke can earn twenty times what we paid for it."

"No, he can't." Chloe gestured at the head of the table. "Bean and I will bring it home."

Graham pointed at her plate. "You might as well stay for breakfast. Bean was right not to let us drive after the duke last night. It *wasn't* safe in all that rain."

Chloe sat back down. "What happened?"

"Faircliffe was in an accident on his way to Mayfair. His curricle was completely destroyed."

She gasped. "Is he... Did he..."

"He's alive," Graham answered. "A fractured bone. His lower leg is in splints. He's still hobbling about his town house, but until he's healed, he won't venture further afield than that."

"Good." Chloe's shoulders slumped back against her chair.

She had no soft feelings for the knavish lord, but she didn't wish him physical harm. The thought that one of her family members could have been driving recklessly after him... She swallowed hard and did not allow her imagination to finish painting the picture.

Bean was *here*.

The entire family was here.

Soon, their heirloom would be home, too.

Technically, an item wasn't an heirloom until one generation inherited it from another. The Wynchesters didn't care about technicalities. They created their own traditions. The *Puck & Family* portrait was already part of their legacy. It would absolutely be handed down for generations... just as soon as they repossessed it from the duke.

Elizabeth sent a glance toward the pile of broadsheets next to Graham's plate. "The morning papers had news of the accident already?"

"Of course not," Tommy said. "Graham's spies are everywhere and far more efficient."

Chloe turned to Jacob. "How are you feeling this morning?"

"Foolish," he admitted. "If I'd kept better hold of my hawk, the duke—"

"It's not your fault *or* your hawk's," Bean said. "The person responsible for the theft is the Duke of Faircliffe."

"I know," Jacob said with a sigh. "But I won't feel whole until we have it back."

"Me neither," murmured the others.

"It's unsettling to see the empty space on the wall," Graham agreed, running a hand over his flyaway black curls.

"Just a faint rectangle where the painting should be." Elizabeth gave a shiver. "Even when I'm not looking at it, I can *feel* it gone."

Chloe put down her fork. "Bean?"

He rose from his seat. "Bring the vase and meet me in the carriage."

Chloe ran upstairs to collect the crystal cherub —how could an ugly vase possibly be equal in value to their painting?—and carefully carried it down the marble stairs and out through the front door, where the family coach awaited.

Rain drizzled from the gloomy clouds. A bit of damp wasn't unusual for England, but the climate had been unseasonably cold and wet ever since Mount Tambora erupted in Indonesia, spewing ash into the air and filling the sky with a haze that stretched over all of Europe. Chloe and everyone else prayed it would pass soon. Crops were beginning to suffer.

Bean wrapped the vase in a blanket and set it at their feet, where it couldn't fall from the seat and be damaged.

"How is your megrim?" she asked.

"It is now a full body ache," he admitted. "I've not been sleeping well, and I likely won't until we've settled this Spranklin Seminary business. I promise to rest once the children are safe and settled."

Chloe didn't like this answer, but neither could she argue with it.

None of the siblings were at peace. This case was too personal. They'd all been orphans once, and they'd all entrusted their lives to a stranger.

Bean was the best father in the world. That sort of luck was unlikely to strike twice. But the thought of being chosen, only to be thrown away all over again...

"Faircliffe residence," Bean informed the driver.

As the coach sprang into motion, Chloe's pulse jittered for a new reason. A better reason. A wonderful reason.

She was en route to the home of her favorite MP.

Yes, yes, the town house was technically his father's home, but it was not the duke who interested Chloe.

It was his son, the Marquess of Lanbrooke.

Bean's blue eyes sharpened. "What is it?"

"Nothing," she said quickly.

His concerned expression did not ease.

"It's just..." How could she explain herself

without making him feel poorly, too? "I love that my ability to blend with the background has helped so many people. I love being an important part of our missions, and I shall never stop doing everything that I can."

"But?" Bean prompted gently.

"Invisibility is a double-edged sword," she admitted. "Being completely unremarkable gives me powers that no one else has, but... it also hurts a little every time."

"Chloe, you're the *opposite* of unremarkable," Bean said. "You're one of the strongest, cleverest, kindest people I've ever had the honor to meet. I wouldn't trade you for the world. You are a treasure."

She tried to smile. "*You* say that, but—"

"Are other people short-sighted? Yes, of course. The world is full of people who don't see the beauty around them. But to the right person, you *won't* be invisible. Your family sees you, do we not? We adore you, just as you are."

Chloe directed her gaze out of the window. She didn't want him to guess that she had a secret tendre for the son of the blackguard who had stolen their family heirloom.

"I'm just worried about our painting," she said.

"We're on our way," Bean said. "*Puck & Family* will be home soon."

He might be surprised to learn that its purchase was the reason Chloe had first become aware of—and interested in—the duke's son. She'd been seventeen the first time she spied on the House of Commons. That year, at the age of twenty-one, it had been Lanbrooke's first session as a Member of Parliament.

She had been fascinated by him. The youngest MP, quite possibly one of the cleverest. He had seemed nothing like the shifty-eyed gambler who'd sold the Wynchesters their adopted family portrait to cover his losses at dice.

Lanbrooke seemed like the sort of person she might like to be friends with.

Or something more.

She'd "accidentally" crossed paths with the handsome orator any number of times over the years. Until now, she'd taken care never to speak to him. What if she'd worked up the courage, and he'd forgotten her just like everyone else always did? Keeping the fantasy was much better than knowing the truth.

"Here we are," said Bean as the carriage pulled to a stop in front of Faircliffe's smart Grosvenor Square town house.

Chloe's pulse beat faster.

"Stay in the coach," said Bean as he leapt to the ground.

Oh. Right. Respectable ladies did not pay uninvited calls upon men, even when they were re-morseless ducal thieves.

"Mind the vase," Bean said. "I'll give you the signal when it's time."

He shut the door.

Chloe brightened, her heart skipping anew. She pulled the vase into her lap and gazed out of the carriage window toward the duke's front door.

In order to maintain her anonymity in case she needed it in the future, she'd never risked speaking to Lanbrooke. As for his father... well. Chloe could apparently dance a jig on the duke's toes and he still wouldn't remember her. He didn't notice her when she was right in front of him.

Would Lanbrooke be different? What would he say when he saw her?

Of *course* he would be different. Wasn't he different from his father in all other aspects? The real question was whether Chloe would have an opportunity to meet him.

Perhaps the duke would exchange the painting for the vase and that would be that. Perhaps the duke would order his *butler* to make the exchange, or his footman, or a maid, and neither man of the house would put in an appearance on the doorstep.

Perhaps—

She frowned and touched the window. Bean was walking back to the carriage. Alone. Empty-handed.

Something had gone wrong.

"What is it?" she blurted out when he stiffly hoisted himself back into the coach.

"The Duke of Faircliffe is a craven knave," Bean replied. "No Wynchesters are to be allowed past the threshold."

"You're not just a *Wynchester*," she stammered. "You're *Baron Vanderbean!*"

It was more than that. Bean *never* returned empty-handed.

Bean leaned his head against the back of the carriage. "Faircliffe's leg is on the mend, but his internal injuries are more dire than first thought."

"The butler told you that?"

"Lanbrooke did." Bean rubbed his temples. "It was part of his *don't-come-back* speech. He says he's no friend of mine, and once his father is gone, I'll have no excuse to return, so I should do us both a favor and stay away."

"What did he say about the painting?"

"He didn't. He shut the door and it would not reopen."

Chloe frowned. Bean always knew exactly what to say to cajole and convince. Perhaps he hadn't pressed because of the accident. "Lanbrooke is preoccupied with his father. If anything ever happened to you, I wouldn't be the least bit rational. We can give him a little time."

"We've no papers of provenance, or *we* could go to the magistrate. Not that they would take any action against a duke." Bean slammed his hand on the seat. "I gave Faircliffe my money and he gave us the painting. It seemed simple. At the time, I didn't care any more than that. After all, we were never going to sell it."

Chloe stared at him in dawning horror. "And now we have no proof that it was ever ours."

"His word against mine," Bean agreed. "And soon, not even that."

She curled her fingers into fists. "What can we do?"

"What we always do," he answered. "Create a plan and execute it."

CHAPTER 5

"*M*iss Chloe? A letter came for you."

Chloe turned from the blank spot on the wall where *Puck & Family* used to be. Their footman, Norbert, stood in the doorway holding a square of parchment.

She strode across the Planning Parlor and unfolded the missive.

SHE'S HERE.
Blond. Pink. Painted fan.

Chloe glanced up at Norbert, startled. "Is this from Mrs. Pine?"

"Yes. Her boy is below."

"Please ask the lad to wait," she told Norbert. "I'll drive him back in the coach."

She dashed to her bedchamber to toss a handful of her new calling cards into a small basket. After pulling on a bonnet and pelisse, she clambered down the steps to the front door.

Bean was already there, handing the boy a shilling in exchange for his secrecy.

He straightened, holding onto his back with one hand. "What's happened?"

"Miss Spranklin is at the orphanage. No doubt hunting a replacement for Dot."

Bean's eyes flashed. "We have to stop her."

"Mrs. Pine isn't the only person who works at the orphanage, but she won't sign over any children," Chloe said. "She'll delay any transactions as long as possible. I can do this part, if you'd like to rest."

"I told you," he replied. "I'll rest when they're all safe."

The coach-and-four pulled up to the door.

"Come along then," Bean said to the wide-eyed boy, motioning him up and into the carriage.

"What's your name?" Chloe asked.

"Henry," answered the boy.

"I'm very pleased to meet you, Henry," she replied. "You did an excellent job of bringing me that letter."

The boy puffed up his chest.

"Do you want to look out of the window?" she asked.

He nodded.

Chloe gave the boy the seat with the best view and arranged herself on the side facing traffic.

"When we get there," she said, "you follow Henry."

Bean frowned. "Where will you go?"

"It's not where I'll go, but who I'll be." She held up a calling card. "This is my opportunity to introduce 'Jane Brown' to Miss Spranklin. It's so much better than turning up on her doorstep. Our meeting will seem completely unplanned. And if I—" Chloe's throat closed.

Bean leaned forward. "What is it?"

"A funeral." She touched the window. "Lanbrooke is in a procession to the cemetery to bury his father."

"Not 'Lanbrooke' anymore," Bean said quietly. "He's the new Duke of Faircliffe."

Faircliffe.

She wondered how long it would take her to remember to call the statesman by his new name. She wondered how long it would take *him* to remember to answer to it.

Poor Lan—er, poor *Faircliffe*.

What an utter nightmare. Chloe would not be surprised if he took some time off from Parliament. She would also not be surprised if he threw himself into his work with even more fervor.

Anything to keep the grief at bay.

"Don't you dare die," she told Bean, her stomach rebelling against the horrific thought.

"We all die," Bean replied, "but I can promise not to take any undue risks. I've no desire to leave you children a single second earlier than I must."

"Look," said Henry. "We're here."

The carriage pulled to a stop at the corner.

"Let me go first." Chloe hopped down to the pavement. "Wait until I'm inside before you follow."

Bean nodded. "I'll teach Henry your magic trick with his new shilling to pass the time."

Henry's eyes widened. "Real magic?"

Chloe flashed a sovereign through her fingers and snapped to make it disappear.

Henry's mouth fell open.

She grinned as she crossed the street to the orphanage. If she guessed right, Henry would practice that trick until he could tilt a coin over and through his fingers with his eyes closed.

When she was perhaps forty yards from the orphanage's front door, an angry-looking woman stalked out wearing a light-pink day dress with dark pink trim, a matching pink spencer, and large bonnet covered in pink silk flowers. The painted fan in her hand beat warm air toward her face, causing her profusion of blond ringlets to bounce in protest.

Miss Spranklin.

It had to be.

Thank goodness she wasn't towing a child behind her. Chloe hurried to catch up.

"Miss Spranklin?" she called out in an upper-class accent. She infused her voice with merriment. "Why, it *is* you!"

The woman paused to look at Chloe, a slight frown flitting across her brow.

It was the expression Chloe's presence always engendered. The vague confidence of having seen a face like hers somewhere before, coupled with a complete inability to produce the name of the person it belonged to.

"Miss Brown," Chloe supplied, then gave a self-deprecating chuckle. "Oh, of course you don't recall my name. I didn't have my cards with me last time, did I?" She made a show of opening her basket and pulling out one of her cards. "Here you are, just as I promised."

Miss Spranklin accepted the card. "'Jane Brown, Governess.' Of course. I remember now."

Whether she was lying to Chloe or to herself was impossible to guess.

Either way, Chloe beamed at her and barreled on, a tornado of bubbly good cheer.

"As you may recall, I tire of being a governess.

I want to be a businesswoman like you! I can barely concentrate from thinking about the empire you've made and the inspiration you are."

Miss Spranklin straightened at this bit of flattery.

"Please say you'll be my mentor and advise me on how best to begin a school of my own. *Or—*" Chloe gasped and clapped her hands together as if the most wonderful idea had occurred to her. "Let me *learn* from you. May I? I could be any kind of assistant you desire. I've the skills of a governess, and I'm not too proud to manage accounts and correspondence or perform any other tasks that need completed. Under your tutelage, I just *know* I'll learn everything there is to know. There's no one I admire more."

That was laying it on a bit thick, but Miss Spranklin had begun to preen more and more with every word.

"I'm in a rush at the moment," Miss Spranklin said, "but if you can pay a call to the school tomorrow afternoon at five, I can spare half an hour in which to give you a proper interview."

The post was as good as Chloe's.

She clasped her hands to her chest. "Oh, *thank* you! You've already been even more marvelous than I dared to dream."

Miss Spranklin's eyes glittered. "I assume you can bring references with you?"

"Of course," Chloe gushed. "It would be *such* an honor to learn from you. I can hardly credit my good fortune. I will be there at five and not a single second late, references in hand. I swear it."

"See that you are," Miss Spranklin said briskly, then turned and strode across the street with a much jauntier gait than when she'd exited the orphanage. She flagged a hackney and was gone with no further delay.

"Good show," said Bean as he and Henry crossed the street to Chloe. "I presume you secured the interview?"

"Tomorrow afternoon," she said with a satisfied smile.

"Watch!" cried Henry.

The shilling managed to tumble across two of his knuckles before slipping through his fingers and falling to the ground.

"Be careful." Chloe scooped it up from the ground and handed it back to him. "That's a magic coin."

"It doesn't seem magic. Every time I—" He stared at the coin in his palm. "It's not a shilling anymore! It's a sovereign! It *is* magic!"

Chloe exchanged a grin with Bean before ushering Henry in through the orphanage door. After presenting their cards to the man guarding the door, she hurried in the opposite direction of the wards toward Mrs. Pine's small office.

The door was closed.

Upon hearing the knock, Mrs. Pine opened the door a crack, then wrenched it open wide.

Dot was seated on the floor in the corner with her arms wrapped about her knees.

"Did you see her?" Mrs. Pine whispered. "Abhorrent woman!"

"I'll find out the extent of it tomorrow," Chloe assured her. "She's allowing me an interview. What did she want here?"

"Nothing that she got!" Mrs. Pine said with a huff. "I caught her wandering the wards without accompaniment, searching for the clever ones just like she did before. This time, I didn't stand for it. I said I knew what she was up to, and told her to keep her grasping hands away from my children!"

No wonder Miss Spranklin had looked incensed.

"What did she say to that?" Chloe asked.

"She smiled a crocodile smile and said, 'Prove it.'" Mrs. Pine's lip curled. "How that woman raises my hackles... She won't be back here, but there are plenty of orphanages to fish from."

"We'll shut her school down," Chloe assured her. "Even if she takes another child in the next week, we shan't leave any behind."

"How?" Mrs. Pine said bleakly. "She's right. We have no proof of wrongdoing, and she can always open another school somewhere else."

"We'll find a way. Evidence is everywhere, if you know where to look. The trouble is knowing where to look. May I have the contract you signed for Agnes?"

"Of course." Mrs. Pine rummaged for a moment then produced a document. "What will it prove?"

"Nothing yet," Chloe admitted. "But it will give us a point of comparison to the contracts signed by the parents whose children *are* receiving a proper education." She sank to the floor next to Dot. "Does any other adult work with Miss Spranklin? Anyone at all?"

Dot shook her head.

"Argh," said Mrs. Pine. "There's no one we can turn against her!"

"No," Chloe said calmly. "This is *good* news. Without an assistant or secretary, Miss Spranklin must deal with administrative tasks herself. Whatever written accounts exist are still there inside the school. And where there's paper..." She snapped her fingers and produced the calling card she'd nicked from Miss Spranklin's reticule. "...I can steal it."

Mrs. Pine covered Dot's ears. "You can steal her ledgers?"

Chloe nodded. "Once I know where to find them."

"I can still hear you," Dot sang out.

"Good." Chloe waved Mrs. Pine's hands away from Dot's ears. "Does Miss Spranklin have an office?"

Dot nodded. "It's locked all of the time, even when she's in it."

Mrs. Pine looked disappointed.

Chloe was thrilled.

"Perfect." She ruffled Dot's hair. "Now we know exactly where to find our evidence. All I have to do is gain access to the office."

"Weren't you listening?" said Mrs. Pine. "The papers are kept under lock and key."

"Pah," said Chloe. "A locked door has never stopped a Wynchester."

CHAPTER 6

"*I*'m fine," Bean insisted. "Or I will be, after I lie down. It may be influenza. You and the others should keep your distance until I recover, so that you don't catch it."

Of course he wouldn't be his usual self whilst fighting influenza. He didn't need her hovering; he needed her patience.

Chloe sighed. "Very well. But if you're not improved in a few days..."

"I'll have a quick rest, and you'll see the difference," he promised.

Troubled, Chloe watched as Bean made his way to his bedchamber with obvious difficulty and closed the door behind him.

Lie down was not something Bean did.

Chloe wasn't certain she had *ever* seen him ill.

She'd suffered influenza a few times herself, so she knew from experience how exhausting it could be. And she knew Bean was getting older. He hadn't been young when he'd rescued her and the others almost twenty years ago. He was old enough to be her grandfather.

"Chloe!" came a loud voice behind her.

She turned to see her sister Marjorie fly down the stairs from her third-floor studio with a sheaf of papers in her hand.

"Six letters of reference," Marjorie announced with pride. "Each written in a different hand on varying qualities and types of paper."

"And if Miss Spranklin writes to these addresses?" Chloe asked as she accepted the small stack.

Marjorie rolled her eyes. "Let her. All of the directions are to far-flung villages nowhere near a stagecoach route. By the time word comes back, we'll have completed the mission."

"Excellent." Chloe tucked the letters into a wicker basket. "See that the kitchen sends up tea and hot soup for Bean. Other than sustenance, he has requested no visitors until he recovers from the influenza."

Marjorie made a face.

"I know," Chloe said. "We all feel the same. Have Graham send for a doctor to be safe. Perhaps the rest of you could stay close, in case Bean needs you?"

"Of course," said Marjorie. "Now go. Don't be late to your interview."

Chloe hurried down the stairs and into the waiting coach. The Wynchester mews contained several types of carriages. This was the one that looked like a common hackney. A governess in search of employment would not arrive in a fancy coach-and-four.

She spent the drive memorizing the contents of Marjorie's letters and inventing histories and anecdotes to go with each. Chloe would be able to answer quickly and easily any question Miss Spranklin might pose about her previous employment.

None of which turned out to be necessary.

The entryway to the Seminary for Girls opened on total chaos.

Miss Spranklin's voice could be heard through an open doorway, calling for order and instructing her pupils to copy whatever she'd just written on her blackboard.

A young servant girl—likely an alleged student —was mopping the corridor. Another stick-thin girl bearing a tea tray had just tripped over the bucket, sending foul water and bits of broken china everywhere.

Several other children abandoned their posts and their studies to investigate the clatter.

Chloe took charge at once.

"You," she commanded one of the girls. "Dry rags, please. You, find a broom. You, pick up the large pieces of china. Perhaps something can be repaired. You, hand me that mop. You, replace the water in this bucket. You and you, back to your studies at once. And you, please stop crying. It is a tea service, not the end of the world."

"B-but the tea," sobbed the miserable girl, "was for *Miss Spranklin*."

"I am certain she is no ogre who would take a simple accident out on an innocent child," Chloe said firmly.

The poor thing. Based on the expression of trepidation in the faces of children who had nothing to do with the accident, Chloe believed the opposite was true. But she'd glimpsed Miss Spranklin approaching from the corner of her eye. The woman would not act against such a positive view of her character.

Not in front of Chloe, anyway.

The girls scattered, either to do Chloe's bidding or because they, too, had seen Miss Spranklin approaching.

"The tea," said Miss Spranklin with obvious displeasure, "was for our interview. I see the cakes are on the floor. It seems we shall have to do without."

Miss Spranklin had ordered the kitchen to

prepare exactly enough cakes for one tea, without any for the children?

"It's no problem at all," Chloe said cheerfully. "I brought cakes enough for everyone."

She opened the lid of her basket and tilted the contents so the others could see the large package inside.

A murmur of excitement rippled through the air.

"What time is the girls' tea?" Chloe asked innocently. "Shall we lay the table now, or should I send the package on to the kitchen?"

Miss Spranklin pursed her lips. "I suppose the pupils may as well have a respite. You and I can talk whilst they enjoy their repast."

As Chloe suspected, Miss Spranklin did not usher all of the girls into the refectory. Only the ones she considered "real" students. The children she used as unpaid servants were to receive nothing at all.

While the headmistress was herding her pupils, Chloe slipped a second package of cakes to the girl who had tripped over the bucket, and whispered for her to go and share it with the others in the scullery.

Once the pupils were settled at the dining table, Miss Spranklin motioned for Chloe to join her in the doorway.

"As you can see," said Miss Spranklin in a

voice low enough to give the impression of discretion yet still loud enough to be heard by the children cleaning the corridor, "this school is sorely lacking in good help."

Chloe gave a sunny smile, as if the comment had been directed at her, rather than the poor children. "When shall I begin?"

Miss Spranklin narrowed her eyes. "How do you do with arithmetic?"

"Quite well. I'm told I have a logical mind."

"And literature?"

"A personal favorite. The best holidays are those spent in the reading room of a lending library."

"Needlepoint?"

"Plain and fancy," Chloe assured her, and hoped she wouldn't be asked to prove it. Tommy was the one who could work magic with needle and thread.

Miss Spranklin harrumphed. "Where are your references?"

Chloe handed her the stack of forgeries at once.

Miss Spranklin began to page through them. "Punctual... responsible... kind but effective disciplinarian... You dealt with our little disruption astutely, I must admit. Children adore you... You've taught everything from writing to—This says you speak French?"

"*Mais oui,*" Chloe said brightly. "*Tout le monde ne le peut pas?*"

"That would ease my load considerably." Miss Spranklin's gaze was calculating. "I suppose you're expecting a king's ransom in exchange for this skill?"

Chloe made her most worshipful expression. "Being able to learn alongside you is worth any wage. Whatever you think is fair, Miss Spranklin. The honor is mine."

A quick, cat-like grin creased Miss Spranklin's face.

"Ten guineas per annum," she said briskly. "And since half of the year is gone, you'll receive five, to be paid in monthly installments at the end of every month."

Ten guineas was what an average under laundry-maid earned.

Miss Spranklin handed the references back to Chloe.

The message was clear: no further questions would be asked about Chloe's qualifications, as long as she accepted a wage that was only a third of what she could earn as a governess.

Chloe clasped her hands together and gave an excited little bounce of joy.

"I shall learn so much from you," she gushed. "When I have my own school, I'll tell everyone I learnt all of the best things from you."

"Don't expect the process to be quick," Miss Spranklin warned. "You might be here for several years before you grasp the details well enough to succeed with a venture of your own."

"I'm sure you're right," Chloe agreed, keeping her expression bright.

Miss Spranklin's eyes narrowed anew. "Were you expecting board as part of these wages? I don't allow any extra souls after nightfall. For the children's safety, of course."

Blast. Nighttime would have been Chloe's best chance to search the school.

"I understand," she murmured in acquiescence. "I will present myself here every morning at the hour you indicate and leave when the work is through."

Miss Spranklin twisted her lips. "Very well. Be here at six every morning, and don't expect to sneak away until six o'clock at night."

Chloe nodded obediently. She retrieved a pencil and leather notebook from her basket and made a show of jotting down Miss Spranklin's instructions.

Tomorrow's basket would contain a few more surprises to slip to the girls.

Mrs. Spranklin strode back to the refectory. "Pupils, your respite is over. Resume your seats and read quietly whilst I give Miss Brown a quick tour of our school."

The girls scrambled to their feet.

At Miss Spranklin's black look, they sat themselves back down at the table and rose quietly as mice, slinking to the schoolroom without a further sound. The headmistress must indeed be a strict disciplinarian if even the favored pupils feared her.

"They're improving," Miss Spranklin assured Chloe. "It's the younger ones that forget their manners whenever there's a distraction. They'll get used to you soon enough. The challenge will be minding their deportment one month from today."

"A month from today?" Chloe repeated, her expression carefully blank.

"It's our annual summer musicale," Miss Spranklin explained, "and the one time per year we allow visitors."

"Parents, you mean?"

"Parents and guardians of current students, yes, as well as prospective students and their parents or guardians. The salon will be overflowing."

No it would not. The Wynchesters would have rescued the girls and shut down the school by then. In a week or so, all of these children would find themselves in far happier circumstances.

"It is of utmost importance," Miss Spranklin was saying, "for the adults to be impressed by what they see at the musicale. It is far easier to keep existing business than to secure new clients, but I have discovered that mingling the current with the new allows our existing parents to promote the school *for* me. The more pleased they are with their child's progress, the more praises they'll sing, and the more likely that the interested parties will sign contracts as well."

That was... clever.

Miss Spranklin was right. Any parent who despaired of educating their child would take one look at these apple-cheeked darlings tapping out melodies at the pianoforte and dream of giving their daughters the same opportunities.

Which meant the boarding school *wasn't* a complete lie.

Miss Spranklin got away with exploiting poor children because she also performed a valuable service for *wealthier* children. The parents who attended musicales and fetched their daughters every year for Christmastide would be pleased indeed with the progress their offspring were making.

And the guardians who dropped off unwanted wards in order to wash their hands of them... would never know just how different the "special" program really was.

"If you'll follow me," said Miss Spranklin. "Down that corridor..."

The visit to the kitchen was quick—a mere

hand wave indicated the washing area and the servants' quarters. The oldest of the unpaid girls was fifteen or sixteen, at best. She ordered the others about briskly and efficiently, but with grammar that indicated her lack of education. All of the children held themselves perfectly stiff at the sight of Miss Spranklin, visibly fearful of giving the headmistress any reason for ire.

Chloe committed the names and features of each child to memory. Many were orphans just like she had been. She would not fail them.

The tour was cursory, and over in less than thirty minutes. Miss Spranklin either did not think Chloe required more detailed information, or else did not wish her students out of her sight for more than half an hour. Chloe glimpsed several closed doors, but with Miss Spranklin at her side, there was no opportunity to try the handles in search of a private office.

"You'll be here at six o'clock tomorrow morning?" Miss Spranklin asked.

Chloe beamed at her. "I wouldn't miss it."

Miss Spranklin gave a sharp nod. "I'll walk you to the door."

"Oh," Chloe exclaimed. "I almost forgot!"

Miss Spranklin turned around, one eyebrow arched. "What is it?"

Chloe handed her a stack of paper. Miss Spranklin accepted the documents reflexively.

Chloe wrapped both of her hands about the handle of her basket so that she could not accept the papers back.

"My references," she said brightly. "I almost carried them back home with me!"

Miss Spranklin gazed down at them as though willing them to disappear. "I'll put them in my office."

She spun away from Chloe, striding back down the corridor and making a sharp left.

Chloe dashed forward silently in order to glimpse which door Miss Spranklin unlocked, then hurried back to her original position before Miss Spranklin came back around the corner, free of Chloe's references.

"Six o'clock," Miss Spranklin said briskly. "You're to begin with French lessons, literature, and composition. I will manage mathematics, comportment, music, dance, and other accomplishments. We will reassess in a fortnight. Perhaps by then, you will be able to take over more of my duties."

On a pittance. Chloe nodded earnestly. "I look forward to it."

She looked forward to shutting the operation down. All the way home, Chloe's heart ached for the terrified children working as unpaid servants. She wished she could tell them it was only for a little while longer, but she could not take the risk.

The rain was sleeting even colder when the carriage reached the Wynchester home. The front door swung open and Graham stumbled outside.

"There you are." His golden bronze features were pale and drawn, his normally springy black curls plastered to his forehead. "The doctor is here."

Chloe's stomach dropped.

Of course the doctor had come. They'd sent for him. He was supposed to inform them that Bean was fine, or would be so shortly. To scold the siblings that their love for Bean had caused them to overreact.

She followed her brother into the house on leaden feet. "Did the doctor say anything?"

Graham closed his eyes and gripped the bottom of the banister to steady himself.

"Smallpox," he whispered.

The wicker basket fell from Chloe's limp hand. "When?" Her voice cracked. "How?"

Her siblings appeared at the foot of the stairs.

"Bean caught it in the past week," Jacob said grimly.

"As for how, you know Bean and his philanthropic visits..." Elizabeth gripped her cane. "He could have been anywhere."

Graham's brown eyes met Chloe's and he gave a wan smile. "The good news is that it is possible to survive smallpox. If anyone is stubborn enough not to die, it's Bean."

"I'm going up to him." Chloe started up the stairs.

Graham caught her arm. "Smallpox's bad humors can linger in the air."

The doctor appeared on the stairs. "You're not to go near there."

"Avoid the sickroom altogether?" Chloe's legs trembled and she gripped the banister tighter. "Stay away from *Bean?*"

"Baron Vanderbean's orders," the doctor said gruffly.

"We're no good to him *or* the orphans if we fall ill, too," Graham murmured.

Chloe's shoulders curved. If Bean didn't want them in the sickroom, then they would honor his wishes. "I'll stay outside the door."

"No," the doctor said. "I recommend avoiding this corridor altogether. Smallpox is highly infectious. I'll need to check all of you, as well. It would be irresponsible and perhaps deadly to put others at risk."

Deadly. Surely he didn't mean— Bean—

"We'll move Bean to the other side of the house until he recovers," Jacob said. "The empty wing shall be a hospital, catering to our patient."

"We?" Chloe repeated.

"Jacob and Marjorie both had smallpox as children," Graham reminded her.

Jacob's case had been light. Marjorie's had left pockmarks on her fair skin and taken away a fair portion of her hearing.

"We've two maids and a footman who are safe to attend him," Elizabeth added. "Bean will be well taken care of."

But not by Chloe. She had been sent home specifically because she could not bear to be far from Bean if he needed her, only to discover she was to be no help at all. The only way Chloe could be of use was by stopping Miss Spranklin.

Chloe touched a hand to her heart and gave a small nod. "For Bean."

CHAPTER 7

Two days later, just before dawn, Chloe and her siblings gathered in the sick wing, in the corridor leading to Bean's closed bedchamber. Their shoulders pressed to the wall separating them from the closest thing most of them had ever had to a father.

Chloe had been the first of the siblings to be adopted and her siblings looked to her for instruction. But she was only the temporary leader. *Bean* was the leader. He was the glue that held the family together. The Wynchesters were who they were because of Bean. They had never spent so much as a single day without him.

"He will be fine," Chloe said firmly.

Her siblings bobbed their heads in agreement, but none of them met each other's gazes.

They'd all lost everything they'd ever had to

lose before. What was to stop Fate from snatching away someone they loved all over again?

Jacob cleared his throat. "Marjorie and I will stay with him."

Marjorie nodded. "We'll read to him, if he feels up to a little company."

Chloe's heart twisted. How she wished she were the one reading to him from his latest novel! Lazy afternoons with a good book had always been a special treat she and Bean had shared.

But she could not be in two places at once, no matter how deeply she wished to.

The children at the Spranklin Seminary needed the Wynchesters' help. Bean would not want them to waste an opportunity to help someone in need.

"The carriage is here," Graham said with obvious reluctance.

Tommy and Chloe pulled away from the wall and trudged down the stairs after their brother.

Chloe had peeked through the sickroom door on several occasions.

The truth was, Bean *didn't* look good. He was covered in horrible pustules.

That was what smallpox *was*, Chloe reminded herself. Plenty of people had scars all over their bodies. It had been painful, but they'd lived through it.

Just because Bean was advanced in age didn't mean...

"Shall we discuss the mission?" Graham said once they bundled into the carriage.

"*Yes*," Chloe said fervently.

It was much better to think about things they *could* change than to dwell on what they could not.

Her siblings looked at her expectantly. It was Bean who guided the planning sessions, Bean who suggested tools and refined strategy.

But until he recovered, it would have to be Chloe. Head of the family for the next fortnight or two, when Bean emerged from the sickroom. She could not let him worry about how things were going without him. The siblings would have to manage without his presence or counsel.

Could they manage without his presence or counsel? What if Chloe missed some detail that Bean would have seen, and they failed to rescue the children before the construction began? What if Bean left the sickbed only to discover Miss Spranklin's newly enlarged boarding school now housed double the quantity of frightened and exploited children?

No. They *had* to save them. For the girls' sake, and for Bean. She straightened her spine.

"Good news." Her voice barely wobbled. "Fortunately, it's an old building with the same style of locks as the orphanage. I could pick them in my sleep."

Her siblings' tight shoulders visibly relaxed. Missions were proceeding as normal, even if their home life was suddenly anything but.

"As soon as I can sneak in, I'll find those contracts," Chloe promised.

"It is deeply satisfying that Miss Spranklin's self-serving greed works in our favor," Graham said. "She tries so hard to take advantage of others, it never occurs to her that others might have ulterior motives, too."

"The bad news is that I scarcely have a moment alone," Chloe said. "The girls are starving for attention and affection. You should see their faces whenever I try to leave them. Somehow, Miss Spranklin always senses when I step away. She materializes right in front of me in the corridor with a new task I'm to add to my repertoire."

Worse, Chloe was making personal connections with each of the girls. The ones taking lessons, and the ones scrubbing dishes and cleaning chamber pots. It felt like the orphanage all over again. The days when Chloe had taught herself to pick pockets in order to buy a crust of bread to share with the others. She had been too young and powerless to save them all back then, but she was grown and capable now. She could not allow her attachment to the children to distract her from doing what must be done to rescue them.

Chloe turned to Graham. "What did you learn from the older girls in the scullery?"

He opened the journal he was keeping for this case.

"It's as we suspected," he said grimly. "The parents whose children are being taught believe their girls to be in a proper school, and have nothing but respect for Miss Spranklin. They think her a stern headmistress, but the girls come from families that believe in discipline, or are also orphans themselves. The guardians are all happy with their choices."

"And the others?" Chloe asked.

His jaw clenched. "The worker girls have no parents, nor proper guardians. They were either foundlings, or orphans dependent upon their parish for charity. The people who sent them to the inexpensive, year-round 'training and placement' program believe they've done well by these girls."

"Believe they've done *well?*" Chloe repeated, appalled. "Terrified six-year-olds engaged in unpaid labor?"

"They don't *know.*" Graham made an expression of disgust. "Miss Spranklin sends progress reports twice a year, and a handwritten note from the girls themselves at Christmastide. I traced a few of the girls' origins and managed to see a sample. The letters home are all far too literate for the age of the child—or the fact that they're receiving no schooling whilst in the scullery."

Marjorie spoke up. "I think the handwriting matches Miss Spranklin's signature on Agnes's admission contract. Miss Spranklin must be writing the letters home herself."

Chloe's fingernails dug into her palms. "That *charlatan*."

"Did you tell them what is happening?" Tommy asked.

"We cannot risk it until we have proof." Graham answered. "I had to pose as a father of one of the children at the school in order to speak to anyone. I could not then confess to not be who I pretended and expect them to believe the unsubstantiated claims of a strange man."

"They'll be horrified when they learn the truth," Chloe said.

A muscle twitched at Graham's temple. "The parishes feel as though they've been charitable and their little problem is dealt with. When the girls turn eighteen, Miss Spranklin sends a note informing each parish that the ward has been placed into gainful, respectable employment and no further progress reports will be forthcoming because she is now independent and self-sufficient."

"*Are* they placed in employment?" Tommy asked.

"I don't know yet," Graham said. "That's what I intend to find out today. Whilst you keep Miss Spranklin and the students occupied, I'll interview a few more of the girls."

Chloe handed him a parcel of cakes from her basket. "Take these to them."

The coach stopped just out of sight of the school to let Graham out of the carriage, and then dropped Chloe off in front of the door.

Miss Spranklin answered with a sly sparkle in her eyes.

"I've had second thoughts," she said as she hurried Chloe inside. "I am responsible for the wise distribution of my pupils' tuition. Why don't you work the first month for free, to ensure that we suit? If we do, I will pay you something extra at Christmastide."

An extra half-penny, perhaps.

No wonder Miss Spranklin worked alone. No one with any sense would accept her selfish, one-sided offers.

Chloe pasted on an earnest expression. "If you think that's best, Miss Spranklin. I'll make a note of it in my journal, so that I remember to do the same one day, just like you."

"Marvelous. Come along, then. I'll send the brightest girls to French instruction with you, whilst I work with the others on their arithmetic. Is that amenable?"

"*C'est parfait*," Chloe assured her.

It was not actually perfect.

What she really wanted was to access Miss Spranklin's office and search for incriminating documents. As soon as Chloe had evidence in hand, they could put a stop to the school's abhorrent practices.

Unfortunately, she was never left alone long enough to do more than visit a chamber pot. Miss Spranklin had an endless list of tasks, and Chloe was assigned to do all of them.

She was exhausted by the time she slumped back onto the squab in the unmarked carriage.

She raised a brow at Graham. "How did you fare with the girls?"

"The cake vanished in an instant." Graham's amusement faded. "The head maid is part of the 'special labor' scholarship. She's frightened of Miss Spranklin, who does not allow any of the girls to leave the school without her permission— which means they have no chance to look for a better opportunity."

"*Paid* employment, for example?" Chloe said dryly. "We *must* get them out of there."

"Some girls *have* left," Graham continued. "Not

when they turn eighteen, as the letters home claim. The girls are gone by the time they're fourteen, once they've shown competence at a skill. Miss Spranklin has successfully placed several girls from the labor program into positions as housemaids, kitchen maids, dairy maids..."

"She *has?*" Chloe said in surprise.

"Don't let it warm your heart too much." Graham's jaw tightened. "Miss Spranklin 'holds' the girls' wages for them in the meantime. They never see a farthing of it."

Chloe clenched her fists. "She deserves to lose every penny."

Graham's brows knitted. "I wonder which bank keeps her money."

"I doubt any bank does," Chloe said. "She can barely leave the girls' sight for more than a few minutes. I'd wager she keeps her riches just as close."

"Such as, inside a certain locked office." Graham smiled. "If you were to stumble across money stolen from innocent girls..."

Chloe grinned at him. "Then we can give the money back to its rightful owners."

CHAPTER 8

*O*n the way home, Chloe and Graham paused to collect flowers in Hyde Park. Like many others, the Wynchester garden at home had suffered terribly with the dreadful weather. Even the greenery of normally lush Hyde Park was limp and sparse.

The sky was a rich blood red. The volcanic haze had lent sunsets an otherworldly hue for months now.

Bean did not attend ton activities, but on summer evenings, when the sun didn't set until after nine o'clock, he often strolled along the Serpentine with Chloe and the other siblings.

She hoped filling his chamber with bright, cheerful clippings would raise his spirits and give him an outing to look forward to, as soon as the smallpox was vanquished and Bean could leave the sickroom again. Perhaps by then, the gloom would have lifted and summer would return.

Chloe held open the lid of her wicker basket so Graham could drop another clipping inside.

"Are these enough?" he asked.

"One more." She lifted her shears. "Perhaps the yellow one, over there by—"

A thundering of hoofs shook the ground.

Everyone walking along the path turned to look as a dashing horse and rider came down Rotten Row.

"*Faircliffe*," Chloe breathed. The new duke looked magnificent.

Graham cut her a sharp look. "That bounder refuses to acknowledge our queries. We've sent countless letters begging for the return of our painting. We even offered to return the vase stuffed with banknotes! He spurns every letter. The butler now shuts the door right in poor Norbert's face."

The new duke was a rude, no-good, very handsome scoundrel. And her greatest hope in the House of Lords for social improvements.

Her *only* hope.

"He's grieving," she reminded Graham and herself. "Can you imagine what that must be like?"

"He replies to *other* people's letters," Graham pointed out. "Other than switching his white cravat for a black one, there's no external differ-ence in his routine. If anything, Faircliffe is as ef-ficient as ever. He's very efficiently decided Wynchesters aren't worth his time."

Chloe clipped the yellow flower. "Perhaps one of us should talk to him in person."

Graham groaned. "We've *tried*. Whilst you are busy infiltrating the school, the rest of us take turns throwing ourselves into Faircliffe's path. He's given me the cut direct so many times, it's a wonder I'm not covered in scars!"

Their breaths caught at the inadvertent re-minder of the damage smallpox would cause to Bean's complexion, and they stared at each other in silence.

Graham swallowed. "I meant..."

"I know what you meant," Chloe said quietly. "And you're right. We need Faircliffe to return our painting *now*, not six months from now when he's finished 'not-mourning.'" She lifted up her basket. "Having *Puck & Family* home where it be-longs will cheer Bean more than a bouquet of flowers."

Faircliffe reappeared, this time going the op-posite direction as before—and much slower.

Graham nudged Chloe forward. "*You* do it."

"*Me?*" Her heart skipped. "I can't. I have to re-tain my anonymity. I—"

Graham plucked the basket from her hands. "Go. Here he is."

Chloe took a deep breath and hurried onto the wide path.

She was not the only one with this idea. Spectators young and old were flocking forward to gawk at the dashing duke.

When he was less than two yards away, Chloe called out, "Your Grace, a quick word if you please!"

His eyes met hers. Bright blue, as brilliant as a sapphire and as fathomless as a summer sky.

Her throat went dry.

Faircliffe lifted his patrician nose and turned his attention back to the road without slowing. By the next heartbeat, all she could see was his back and his horse's arse.

Graham bared his teeth. "Cold as ice. Now you see what we've been up against."

Chloe wasn't certain which possibility was worse: that Faircliffe rebuffed her on sight without even knowing who she was, or that he *had* known who she was and she'd never even realized it.

"It's not you, darling," said an older lady who clearly did not know Chloe was a Wynchester. "Mrs. York has picked him out for her daughter Philippa. I'm afraid none of you other girls have a chance."

The older woman patted Chloe on the arm and continued down the walking path.

"That was simultaneously comforting and rude," Chloe muttered to Graham. "And who the devil is Philippa?"

"Miss Philippa York," said Graham, "age two and twenty, and the only child of Mr. and Mrs. Lester York of Grosvenor Square, directly opposite the Faircliffe town house."

"Wait," Chloe said. "Mr. York, of the House of Commons?"

"The very one. Although his daughter is on her fourth season and has been labeled a bluestocking, Miss York is celebrated as a paragon of charity and selfless good works."

"She sounds splendid," Chloe said sourly.

"She also has the largest dowry on the marriage mart," Graham added.

"If she's perfect *and* rich, why isn't she married?"

He pointed at the hoof prints from Faircliffe's ride past. "She's received countless offers. The Yorks will only accept a title, and their eye is on that one."

Wonderful.

Chloe wagered that when the Duke of Faircliffe looked at lovely, wealthy Philippa York, he didn't look right through her as he passed by.

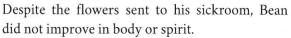

Despite the flowers sent to his sickroom, Bean did not improve in body or spirit.

He needed something better. Something bigger. He needed Chloe to save the orphans and produce the family painting. She'd failed to make progress with Faircliffe at Hyde Park, but she would not fail the girls at Miss Spranklin's school.

Today, she would break into the office and find the evidence that would free the exploited children from Miss Spranklin's control.

Chloe had a plan. She *had* to create the plans. Bean could not craft stratagems for them. So she'd created a Bean-worthy plan that would make him proud when she returned victorious.

The rest of her siblings were at home. Not *in* Bean's sickroom, but close enough to hear him if he were to call for them. Thus far, he was too unwell to call for anyone, but the moment he was better, they wanted to be right by his side.

Her carriage pulled to a stop in front of the school. Chloe picked up her umbrella, looped her basket over her arm, and hurried up the path to the main door.

Did her siblings think she didn't love Bean as much as they did because she hadn't canceled all other obligations? She was here at the school instead of home with Bean *because* rescuing children was the best way Chloe could show him that she cared, she understood, she had learnt everything he'd taught her and would put those in need over her own fears and heartbreak.

If she stayed home doing nothing, just waiting, waiting, waiting outside of Bean's door for a sign that he was improving, any sign at all, she would be a lifeless puddle from the stress and worry.

Taking action was better. Solving problems was better. Making Bean proud was better.

"Six o'clock exactly," Miss Spranklin said coldly as Chloe shook off her umbrella in the doorway. "When I say six o'clock, I mean for you to be ready to work at that hour, not fussing with your bonnet and pelisse. See that it doesn't happen again."

"Yes, Miss Spranklin," Chloe said meekly.

If Elizabeth were here, she'd stab Miss Spranklin with her umbrella.

Jacob would release a pack of wild ferrets.

"Go on, then," said the headmistress. "French lessons for an hour with your set, whilst I teach mine their songs for the musicale in the salon."

"Yes, Miss Spranklin," Chloe said again, and hurried into her classroom.

A dozen little girls sat ramrod straight in wooden chairs, hands folded in their laps, heads bowed, their nervous gazes fixed on the table before them.

Chloe shut the door. "It's me."

A palpable sense of relief spread through the room, dissipating the tension from the air. The girls lifted their gazes and smiled trustingly at Chloe. She taught them French with games and songs and encouragement. She did not berate them for mistakes or reprimand them with a ruler. She treated them like fellow human beings.

"Today," Chloe announced, "I have a special treat. *Two* special treats."

She placed her basket at the end of the table and opened the wicker lid. Inside the basket were oatcakes and raisin biscuits, as well as a tall stack of parchment. Chloe had spent all night drafting the perfect papers for her students to work on independently, tailoring each task to the child and her level. Conjugations and composition for the eldest, matching and copying for the youngest. Between the practice work and the sweets, the girls would be busy for an entire hour.

Chloe was counting on it.

She handed out the papers and explained the instructions. "For each page you complete, you are allowed to select *one* cake or biscuit from the basket. Understand?"

Never had a group of girls been so delighted to receive a stack of coursework.

"Where will you be?" asked Nettie, one of the older pupils.

Chloe held up a brown paper package. "I shall deliver these to the girls in the scullery, and then return posthaste. I trust you will all remain silent and studious while I am gone?"

The children's eyes widened, and they nodded vigorously. They did not want to catch Miss Spranklin's attention any more than Chloe did.

"Off you go, then. Attend to both sides of page one before you select a biscuit."

A dozen pencils immediately flew to the first page.

Chloe cracked open the door and listened for the sound of music coming from the salon before she slipped out into the corridor.

One hour. An abundance of time. She had once picked pockets without breaking her stride. Picking locks was only a tiny bit slower. Finding damning evidence and misappropriated wages... well, she would cross that bridge once she was inside Miss Spranklin's office.

But first, she had to deliver the cakes to the scullery. If Chloe were caught with them, Miss Spranklin would see that the poor overworked girls never received a single crumb. Chloe didn't *think* Miss Spranklin would dismiss her for an insubordination this innocuous, but she didn't want to find out.

Chloe hurried down the corridors to the kitchen and scullery at the rear of the school. She had been slipping the girls packages of food whenever she could. They even had a secret spot behind the potatoes where they hid their bounty.

It hurt Chloe's heart that the children couldn't openly enjoy something as simple as a raisin biscuit. But she was here to solve that problem. Today. This very morning.

"Thank you so much," gushed the girls. "Will you stay and share one with us?"

"I would love to, but I really—" Chloe's stomach twisted at their crestfallen expressions. "Just one. I must hurry back to my class."

She hated to abruptly abandon such lonely, eager-to-please children, but her hour in which she could help them was already dwindling precipitously. As soon as she could do so without hurting their feelings, Chloe hurried back into the corridor and made her way to Miss Spranklin's office.

Distant music from the pianoforte drifted down the hall. Chloe checked her pocket watch. *Fifteen minutes* remaining? Her fingers shook. She could manage it. She *had* to.

She returned her watch to her pocket and pulled out her picks. She dropped to one knee in order to be at eye level with the keyhole as she twisted her metal rods this way and that.

Only when the *click* of the interior mechanism falling into place sounded clear and sharp did

Chloe realize the pianoforte in the salon had gone quiet. She grabbed her watch. She still had ten minutes! Miss Spranklin would not have ended lessons early for any reason.

Of course she would. She was Miss Spranklin. The one game she enjoyed just as much as terrorizing children was appearing unexpectedly to check on Chloe.

Cursing under her breath, Chloe used her picks to push the pins back into a locked position and then sprinted down the corridor and around the corner to her students' classroom. Her hand had barely closed on the door handle when Miss Spranklin's footsteps sounded from the opposite direction.

"Going somewhere?" came the headmistress's sharp voice.

Going somewhere. Perfect. Miss Spranklin thought Chloe was sneaking *out* of her classroom, not back into it. She spun to face the headmistress.

"I heard the music stop ahead of schedule," Chloe said brightly, "and worried something had happened and that you might need me. Is there anything I can do to help you?"

"Doubtful," Miss Spranklin said. "Unless you're particularly gifted at finding missing children."

Chloe gave her a blank look. "Missing... children?"

"A runaway." Miss Spranklin crumpled what appeared to be a letter in her fist. "I hired a man to search a five-mile radius of the school, and he's come up empty-handed. I've sent him to interview the orphanage Dorothy came from."

Dot. Chloe's stomach dropped. "If there are no angry parents to consider, must you waste your hard-earned money on an investigator?"

Chloe would spare no expense to find a missing child, but Miss Spranklin did not seem the sort to spend a single farthing. England was overflowing with orphans and foundlings. Why did Miss Spranklin care about Dot?

"I won't have a child undermine my control," the headmistress snapped. "*Especially* a chit who was only here for a month. I shall make an example of her when she returns, and no other girl will dare go against my command."

"I see," Chloe murmured. Of course Miss Spranklin wouldn't want the children to have hope of one day escaping her control. She liked to keep everyone under her thumb.

Miss Spranklin's lip curled. "There's an old woman at the orphanage whom I don't trust a bit. Perhaps I ought to send the investigator there. Miss Brown, I need you to take over mathematics and music whilst I plan—"

"Take over your duties as well? I have no *time* for that!" Chloe burst out.

"I'll increase your gift at Christmastide."

There *was* no Christmastide. There was Bean, erupting in painful pustules at home, waiting for Chloe to bring word of a successful mission, which *might* have happened if everything didn't aspire to sap away the precious few moments she had in which to *achieve* the mission. And now Miss Spranklin wanted Chloe to be even more occupied, whilst the headmistress shuttered herself inside the one and only room that held the key to escaping this hell?

"I don't want your money." To Chloe's horror, her eyes shimmered and her voice broke. "I have —my father is very ill and—I cannot prepare more coursework than I already—I never know what condition I'll find him in when I—"

"I can see you're of no use to me in *your* condition," Miss Spranklin said coldly. "Go home, Miss Brown. Take the rest of the day. I will dock it from your wages. But I expect you back here at a quarter to six tomorrow morning with none of this blubbering. Is that understood?"

"No—I—"

"At once, Miss Brown. It is an order. Do not question me again." Miss Spranklin lifted a brow.

Chloe had no choice but to nod dutifully, retrieve her now-empty basket, and slink out into the rain to flag down her carriage.

Should she have stayed? People were counting on her. *Everyone* was counting on her. Bean, the girls, her siblings. Chloe was letting them all down by falling apart. She *had* to win out. There was no other possibility. And she had to stop crying before her red eyes gave her away in front of Bean.

If anything happened to him while Chloe was playing handmaiden to Miss Spranklin...

As soon as the carriage paused in front of the Wynchester home, Chloe raced upstairs to the sick wing, hoping assure herself Bean was doing fine and was on the mend.

The doctor blocked her path. He closed the sickroom door behind him and herded her further down the corridor toward the rest of her siblings, well away from Bean's door.

"It's for your own good," the doctor said gently. "Our patient is very ill and would be deeply upset if any of you were to catch smallpox from him."

"I know," Chloe said in a defeated voice. "I just... miss him."

Tommy nodded, her normally animated face pale and splotchy. She was barred from visiting Bean too, until he recovered.

"When will he be better?" Elizabeth asked,

leaning heavily on her cane. The distress of Bean's illness and not being able to see him must be causing Elizabeth's chronic pain to intensify.

For a moment, there was no reply.

"Miss Elizabeth," the doctor said gently. "Baron Vanderbean's fever has worsened. He's developed lesions on his throat."

Chloe's breath caught.

"What is he saying?" Tommy swung wild eyes toward Chloe. *What is he saying?*

"Please do not panic," said the doctor. "Not yet. I'll return in the morning."

When the doctor's footsteps faded down the stairs, all six siblings touched their fingertips to the wall where Bean fought for his life on the other side.

"I promise we'll save the children," Chloe said fiercely.

"And I promise we'll get our painting back," Tommy added. "Whatever it takes."

"Please get better," Jacob whispered.

CHAPTER 9

*A*t four o'clock the next morning, Chloe lurked outside the Palace of Westminster. It was the end of June and ostensibly summer, but instead of the bright yellow and pink of dawn, the gloom stretched over the entire city. No, the entire country. The weather was worse day by day, growing colder and hazier and wetter and darker.

She would not be here at all, except that it was the waning weeks of the House of Lords, making it her last opportunity to intercept the Duke of Faircliffe and beg for the return of the Wynchester family portrait.

Chloe would not be allowed to enter the sickroom triumphant to show Bean their painting had returned, but she *would* be the one who brought the heirloom back home.

Parliament ended anywhere between midnight and the wee hours of the morning. Chloe had been standing here, beneath a sodden umbrella, since eleven o'clock. The carriage was at the corner, with the driver asleep inside. She could have waited there, out of the rain, but she didn't want to miss her chance to speak to Faircliffe.

Bean needed their painting to come home where it belonged. If they could hang it in his sickroom, it would give him strength. His beloved sprites would be there on his wall, even if they were barred from his chamber in person. If it was the closest Chloe could come, then she was determined Bean would have it.

The doors swung open and clumps of expensively tailored lords spilled out of the palace.

She waited in the shadows until she saw Faircliffe.

He walked alone.

This was her moment.

She rushed forward. "Your Grace! My apologies for the other day at Rotten Row. If you could give me just *one* moment of your time, my family will very much make it worth your—"

He stepped around her and continued walking.

Her mouth fell open.

Of all the—

"Who was that chit?" she heard another lord ask him.

"What?" the duke replied blankly. "Where?"

That arse!

He climbed into his waiting carriage without bothering to look behind him.

Chloe closed her jaw with an audible click and tried to ignore the heat pricking at the back of her eyes.

She'd been right in front of him. *Talking* to the blackguard. He'd had to physically move aside in order to brush past her and continue on.

And she had *still* left no memory of her presence behind.

Chloe hugged herself, fists clenched, as she trudged back to her waiting carriage.

"I cannot believe I thought delivering your vase would ruin my anonymity," she muttered under her breath. "I could break it on your head, and you wouldn't notice."

She recognized the irony. Being wholly unremarkable was a skill she'd cultivated for decades. Invisibility gave her *power*.

Yet lately, all she felt was powerless.

After spending another fruitless day trying and failing to sneak into Miss Spranklin's office with the headmistress unawares, the next evening Chloe met her siblings in the corridor leading to the empty wing with Bean's sickroom.

The doctor was inside.

"Did you—" Elizabeth began.

Chloe shook her head. "I'll try again tomorrow."

"You don't have to," Jacob said. "Tell Miss Spranklin you need a few days, and you'll return when Bean is better."

"I do have to." Chloe's words came out wooden and hollow. "I'm not like you. I can't visit Bean and read to him from his sickroom. Stopping Miss Spranklin is the only thing I *can* do."

"But you're not," Marjorie said.

"I'm trying to!" Chloe burst out, her voice shaking. "You have no idea what it's like to have two dozen frightened little girls clinging to your limbs whilst trying to dodge a headmistress whose favorite activities are 'looming over one's shoulder' and 'popping up out of nowhere' and making me—"

"That *is* what Marjorie means," Jacob said gently. "It's an impossible task under the best of circumstances, and that is not where we find ourselves. 'Chloe in top form' can do anything, but 'Chloe worried sick about Bean' will not be able to concentrate properly. You can't help the girls in this condition."

"I can't help Bean either," Chloe said wretchedly. "I make it as far as the office door and I'm stopped. I place myself in front of Faircliffe, and I'm brushed aside. Even if it's hopeless, shouldn't I keep trying?"

"Not if it makes you sick, too." Elizabeth leaned on her sword stick. "You'll be of no help to anyone. You're driving yourself mad, Chloe. When is the last time you slept? You spend all night copying papers, then long hours standing in the rain outside of Westminster. You look terrible. If you keep this up, you'll be in a sickbed of your own. Do you think that's what Bean wants?"

Chloe looked into the faces of one concerned sibling after another, then slumped her shoulders against the wall. She *hadn't* been sleeping. There was too much to do. Too many people who needed her.

But Elizabeth was right. Chloe's brain was now sluggish, and too full of concern about Bean to concentrate on much else, no matter how hard she tried. Her reaction times were slower, her fingers shaky with the picks, her usually glib alibis choppy and suspicious. She was not helping Bean.

She wasn't helping anyone.

"You're right." Chloe swallowed. "Family comes first. I'll pen a letter to Miss Spranklin telling her I need a few days and she's welcome to dock an entire month from my wages. She'll lecture me, but she won't say no."

"It's the right choice," Jacob said. "When Bean's better, *you'll* be better, and we'll be able to get justice for those poor girls."

Chloe nodded. "As soon as I can see Bean again, I—"

The sickroom door opened, and the doctor emerged.

His face was grave.

"No," Elizabeth whispered.

Chloe's flesh turned cold and clammy. "Is... Is he..."

"He's alive," the doctor said carefully, "but he's not eating. His vision is impaired, which may be permanent, but the most concerning—"

"*No,*" Tommy interrupted before the doctor could finish his sentence. "Bean *promised* he would recover."

The doctor's eyes were sad, but he closed his mouth. There was nothing more to say.

"No. He'll be fine." Chloe linked arms with her sister and ignored the scratchy thickening of her throat. "Bean loves us too much to die."

"*Ices,*" Chloe said decisively the following evening as she and her siblings stood before Gunter's pineapple sign. "Bean must eat to regain his strength. He adores fresh fruit ices. They'll feel good on his poor throat and taste like better times."

She didn't say that she was doing this because it was the only thing she could do. She was no good at the school or with Faircliffe, but she could cheer up Bean, and perhaps her siblings too, while she was at it.

They were all desperate to feel useful. Desperate to have hope again. This was a task they could achieve. Something tangibly good they could do for Bean.

Chloe dragged in an uneven breath and tried to portray confidence. This had to work.

Jacob nodded. "We'll buy all of his favorite flavors."

They carried china serving dishes with deep lids filled with ice that would help keep the contents cold until they could get home.

"For Bean," Chloe said firmly.

All six siblings touched their free hand to their hearts. "For Bean."

After purchasing as much flavored ice as would fit into the china, Chloe led them out of the door toward the carriage. She ran straight into the Duke of Faircliffe and almost dropped her china pail.

"*You*," she snarled before he could move out of

the way. "Give us back our painting, you cad. You cannot ignore us when we're right in front of your—"

The duke turned sideways to slip between Marjorie and Elizabeth and entered the tea shop without looking back.

"That unmitigated bloody bounder!" Chloe sputtered. "I will swing this pail right into his pretty face, and *then* we'll see if that haughty, glacier-hearted bastard notices me!"

"We'll destroy him later," Jacob said. "Bean needs us."

Determined that this treat would bring comfort and good cheer at last, the Wynchesters entered their home carefully cradling Bean's favorite flavors of ice. They waved away help from the butler and carried their china dishes to the sick wing.

The doctor met the siblings on the steps.

Chloe's lungs caught.

The doctor's eyes went soft at the sight of them. He shook his head.

"*No,*" was all that scratched from her throat.

The doctor's kind face was full of sympathy. He let out a sigh. "Wynchester family, I am very sorry to inform you—"

They hadn't even been *here*.

The china fell from Chloe's hand.

The dishes fell from all of her siblings' hands. Shards of fine china splattered in brightly colored patches of Bean's favorite ices all over the floor. The Wynchesters found each other, their arms wrapped around each other so tight it was impossible to tell where one's tears ended, and another's began.

Not Bean.

The unthinkable had happened.

There would be no more strolls with Bean in Hyde Park, no visits to Gunter's *en famille*, no lazy afternoons side-by-side with Bean with a good book, no more late-night sessions in the Planning Parlor as Bean outlined a clever new scheme, no more hugs when Chloe pulled off the impossible, no ceremonial re-hanging of the family portrait, followed by arranging themselves in their usual order with Bean at the center of the family.

He wouldn't be in the center anymore. He wouldn't be there at all.

Bean was gone.

Forever.

CHAPTER 10

*T*hat Sunday, Chloe and her siblings sat side-by-side in a single pew. Alone in the cavernous church save for a few close friends, one solemn clergyman, and an elm coffin with a silver plate engraved with flowers and angels.

Although the other pews only contained Mrs. Pine and a handful of Bean's dearest friends, it felt like too much to take. Their presence made Bean's absence *real* in a way Chloe could hardly bear to contemplate.

She had thought if they avoided the outside world, if she didn't have to talk about Bean's death, if she didn't have to admit the truth, then maybe she could pretend for a little while longer that they weren't going to dig a hole in the earth and bury Bean inside.

The Wynchesters were renowned for their ability to solve impossible missions. Yet here they were, broken. Unable to mend the most important mistake of all. Unable to bring back the person they loved most, the first person to love all of them and give them a home and a family.

Chloe couldn't bear to have strangers see her like this. Even worse would be to have people they knew catch them with tears on their faces, small and defeated.

No one loved Bean as much as they did. Most appreciated him, respected him, were grateful to him, though there were a few who felt Bean hadn't minded his place. Was too eager to poke his nose in where it wasn't wanted and try to solve other people's problems for them.

Smallpox was the one villain even Bean could not vanquish.

Some lords of the ton were resentful of Bean's success. A rich foreigner achieving whatever he pleased, whilst they stared at their empty coffers. They outranked him with their English titles but were not better men. Those shriveled souls would not be sorry Bean was gone.

Chloe was glad she and her commoner siblings need have nothing to do with a Polite Society like that.

They didn't understand that to the Wynchesters, Bean wasn't *like* a father. He *was* their father. Who cared if he wasn't a nobleman? He was the greatest man they'd ever known. He'd given them

more than a home. He'd given them unconditional love, a battle to fight, and the skills and
means with which to help others. What could be
more noble than that?

Bean turned them into a family in every way
that mattered. They weren't all alone anymore.
They were a cohesive group. Part of a team,
with Bean as the fearless, indomitable
leader who—

No. He was not the leader anymore. They
were no longer a cohesive group. They were six
orphans, orphaned all over again, with a hole in
their hearts and their home that no amount of
time or money could ever fill. The person they
most wished to cling to was about to be taken
away forever.

It was time.

A rustle sounded in the rear of the black-
draped church, as pages and bearers cloaked in
black presented themselves. The funeral train
would proceed to St. George's Gardens for the
burial service.

To bury *Bean*. In the dirt. And cover him with
a heavy stone.

Chloe squeezed Marjorie's hand.

"The gentlemen will now accompany Baron
Vanderbean to his final resting place," said the
clergyman, Mr. Hartwell. "Ladies, a carriage will
take you home."

All six siblings rose to their feet, but they did not divide into two directions.

They kept together as they exited the church, turning as one toward the elegant all-black processional coaches engaged to transport the deceased and his mourners to the cemetery. A pair of pure black horses pulled each carriage, with somber plumes of black ostrich feathers rising from each horse's head-dress.

"Ladies," Mr. Hartwell said more emphatically, "I am certain your delicate sensibilities cannot manage a burial ceremony. That is why women do not attend funerals."

"I'd like to see you stop us," Elizabeth growled.

Startled, Mr. Hartwell took a step back and allowed them to continue.

Marjorie, Chloe, and Elizabeth were dressed in black crape mourning gowns, shawls and gloves. Tommy was dressed in the same black gentlemen's attire as her brothers. Clouds draped the sky in black, the air cold and thick with impending rain.

Once Bean was tucked safely into the hearse, the funeral furnisher, Mr. Quincey, turned to the siblings, his voice thick with emotion.

"My family business would not exist if Baron Vanderbean had not helped my father when he needed aid most." Mr. Quincey's voice cracked.

"We are forever grateful to him. He was one of the best men I have ever known."

That sounded exactly like Bean.

The siblings exchanged shimmering glances.

Mr. Quincey cleared his throat. "You will not be receiving a bill for these services. Thanks to your father, our business is more profitable than we dreamed."

"Nonetheless, you deserve compensation for your labor," Jacob said. "Bean would not want us to take advantage of anyone. Please let us pay you in his honor."

"We thank you for your kind offer and all of your effort," Chloe added. "If ever you need anything, please don't hesitate to come to us. We are at your service, just as Bean was."

Mr. Quincey gave a jerky nod. "I wouldn't expect less from a Wynchester," he said gruffly. "No one has ever heard you say no to someone in need."

He turned before they could respond and strode further down the processional to guide the attendants into their carriages.

Isaiah, their black-liveried tiger, helped Chloe into the coach meant for the Wynchesters. The six siblings settled themselves in the same order as their family portrait.

Just like the portrait, Bean was missing.

The painting would come home. The Wynchesters would see to that. But Bean never would. He'd been stolen from them permanently.

They exchanged bleak glances.

"I should have been there for him," Chloe blurted out. "Not teaching French, five miles away—"

"I never left the house," said Elizabeth, "and I couldn't see him either. We were banned from the sickroom."

"Protecting us," Graham said, his voice rough. "Down to his last breath."

"So very Bean," Tommy said softly. "A Puckish angel to the end."

Bells were ringing as they filed out of the carriage. A cold rain had begun to fall.

The siblings followed the coffin to a large hole in the earth. Jacob, Graham, and Tommy joined the pall-bearers. Elizabeth, Chloe, and Marjorie hung behind.

Chloe couldn't look at the coffin. Didn't want to see her siblings and the other pall-bearers lower Bean into a gaping hole or pile dirt on top of him.

Just knowing it was going to happen compressed her stomach into a tiny little ball.

But she couldn't walk away from Bean until she absolutely had to. He had never left Chloe behind. It hurt to abandon him.

Mr. Hartwell began the funeral sermon.

She tried not to think what life would be like without Bean. He'd provided well for them, of course. He always did.

Years ago, he'd created "Horace" and "Honoria," his fictitious heir and heiress. A baron, even one from Balcovia, a small foreign principality in the Low Countries, had far more status than a group of orphans. Avenues that were denied to Chloe and her siblings welcomed Horace and Honoria with open arms. It gave them access they would not otherwise have.

Whilst Bean was alive, they'd had little use for the fiction, but now that he was gone, that, too, would have to change. Marjorie would teach the siblings how to forge the supposed heir and heiress's signatures. If a personal appearance was required, Tommy could impersonate either Horace or Honoria. Bean would no longer be there to sweep in and save the day. But they weren't completely on their own.

Bean had made additional bequests.

He'd provided small fortunes for all of them. Each would earn a respectable annuity in the five-percents. Not that the siblings needed the money. Bean's will stipulated that every expense would be fully covered, for any sibling or any client.

He had also created an even larger trust, the interest of which was to be used for orphans.

That was the entire direction: *For orphans.* The "how" was up to the Wynchesters.

Chloe shifted her weight on the uneven grass.

Countless other sums had gone to this person or that charity, with a generous annuity set aside for each of the servants.

And he'd left the novel he was currently reading… to Chloe.

Her eyes grew moist and a crooked smile came unbidden to her lips. He hadn't mentioned the novel by name. The testament had been written years before he'd fallen ill. But Bean had been confident he and Chloe would still be reading together and exchanging books.

He was sharing his with her one last time.

A loud sniff behind her caused Chloe to glance over her shoulder. She jumped, startled.

The cemetery was no longer empty. The small family-only service was now flanked by a growing crowd.

The mourners were all of the people Bean had helped over the decades. From titled peers to working people who had interacted with him and come away the richer for it.

Chloe exchanged awed glances with her siblings. They had only told a handful of close friends, but word had got out, perhaps through the funeral furnisher's staff or those at the church. The silent support was overwhelming. It was as though all of these people were saying, *We loved him, too.*

We feel your pain.

You are not alone.

As soon as the service ended, they came one by one to pay their respects. Mrs. Pine enveloped her in a fierce hug. It was almost Chloe's undoing.

"I'm sorry I stopped going to the school," she choked against Mrs. Pine's maternal shoulder. "I've not forgotten Dot or the other girls. We *will* rescue them. I promise."

"I know you will." Mrs. Pine hugged Chloe harder. "I have never doubted you for even a moment."

When the final flower had been laid and the last mourner was gone, the six Wynchester siblings were alone once again.

They hovered in a protective circle around Bean's grave as the final bells rang.

"Goodbye, Bean," Tommy said quietly. "I love you."

"I'll miss you forever," whispered Elizabeth.

"We all will." Graham's voice was rough.

"We'll get our painting back," Chloe vowed. "*Puck & Family* will be reunited again, I swear it."

"No matter what it takes," Marjorie agreed fervently.

"But first," said Jacob, "we'll save the children, just as we promised we would."

Graham nodded and swallowed. "We do it for Bean."

They touched their hands to their hearts, then lifted their fingers to the sky, where the closest man they'd ever had to a father must be smiling down on them with pride.

"For Bean!" they chorused as one.

They met each other's eyes.

It was time to plan a rescue.

CHAPTER 11

*O*ne week later, Chloe strode into her house with her bonnet a sodden mess and her lips pressed tight.

Elizabeth leaned on her sword stick. "No?"

"*No*," Chloe growled.

Ever since she'd returned from her "unauthorized holiday," Miss Spranklin had been more demanding than ever. There was rarely an opportunity for Chloe to dash to the necessary, much less break into Miss Spranklin's office at the opposite side of the school.

With the aid of several glowing—if forged—personal recommendations, Tommy had managed to infiltrate the school as a "hired" dancing-master, on condition that she provide the headmistress with the first fortnight of services for free in order to prove her skills.

Chloe hoped Miss Spranklin's greed would

give Tommy opportunities to distract her so Chloe could break into the study.

Jacob poked his head over the staircase banister and called, "Come up to the Planning Parlor."

Tommy handed the butler her coat and top hat, then followed Chloe and Elizabeth up the stairs.

The Planning Parlor didn't feel the same without Bean. His chair was empty. The space on the wall where the family portrait should be was empty.

Chloe wouldn't think about any of that. She had sworn to Bean that she would put a stop to Miss Spranklin's abhorrent practices, and Chloe fully intended to keep that promise.

"Another hard day at work?" Jacob asked.

She looked at him sharply. What had he meant by that? Was it an innocuous question? Or did sweet, sensitive Jacob think less of Chloe because she was still getting up and doing what must be done, despite slogging through a whirlpool of grief?

Chloe struggled with the answers to those questions. Every time she presented herself at the school, she wondered if she should be able to. If she was upset enough. If she truly loved Bean and missed him as much as her siblings did, wouldn't she be home in her bed, unable to face the day?

But every morning when she stared up at her canopy, tempted to pull the covers over her head and stay underneath until the darkness finally passed, she told herself this was how she *proved* she loved Bean. By functioning. By carrying on. By doing the things he was no longer here to do but would have had faith that she could manage.

She wouldn't disappoint him. Not then, and not now.

Once the girls employed with garnished wages were free of their unethical contracts, once the children forced to labor as unpaid servants were out from under Miss Spranklin's unyielding thumb, *then* Chloe would take a breath.

But only then. Only when she kept her promise to Bean.

Marjorie entered the Planning Parlor and took her seat next to Elizabeth.

Chloe frowned. "Where's Graham?"

Jacob shrugged. "Out."

"He's gone all day just as long as you and Tommy," Elizabeth said. "Sometimes longer."

Chloe lifted a shoulder. "He'll be here. Let's get started."

"Did you find anything at the school?" Jacob asked.

"No," Chloe answered. "Getting Tommy hired is a double-edged sword. Now there are two of us with an excuse to roam the corridors. But in exchange for that access, Miss Spranklin now has more free time to spend in her office—which is where we want to be."

"How will you get her out of there?" Elizabeth asked.

"We can't," Tommy said simply. "We've tried everything. She's either breathing down our necks or locking herself inside the room we need to break into."

"Which gives us no choice," Chloe finished, "but to switch plans to our contingency."

Marjorie made a face. "Musicale?"

Chloe nodded grimly. "Musicale."

"It adds a lot of risk factors," Elizabeth said slowly. "More witnesses—"

"Adult witnesses," Jacob added.

"—a tight timeline—"

"One and a half hours exactly," Tommy confirmed. "Not all of the girls have a song they can play at the pianoforte."

"—a chaotic environment..." Elizabeth continued.

"Precisely what we're counting on," Chloe said. "Miss Spranklin will be holding court in the main salon at the front of the building. She is the face of the school. She *must* be there to reassure parents and coax money out of prospective clients."

"This is our one chance," Tommy said. "We

will have ninety minutes. We have to make each moment count. And we need to cover Chloe so she can sneak out of the salon."

Her siblings nodded. "Just tell us what to do."

Chloe's chest filled with pride. A Wynchester never gave up just because the odds were impossible. A Wynchester did the impossible anyway.

"We have two days to prepare," Chloe began. "Tommy will be on the dais with Miss Spranklin. The headmistress wishes to show off and will dance a short reel with Tommy and the elder children whilst the most competent musician plays her piece at the pianoforte."

"I'm the first line of defense," Tommy explained. "I'll be physically closest to Miss Spranklin, therefore best able to distract her from noticing Chloe's absence."

"But she's tricky," Chloe continued. "Which is why we need Elizabeth to—"

Graham burst through the door with his cravat askew and his black curls in disarray, likely from being smushed beneath a top hat for unknown hours.

"Where were you?" Marjorie asked.

"In Benson." He flopped into his armchair. "I tracked down—"

"You went to *Benson* and back?" Jacob repeated. "In one day?"

Elizabeth arched a brow. "I thought you said

Faircliffe was a horrid human for becoming *more* efficient after his father's death."

"Faircliffe *is* a horrid human," Graham muttered. "But maybe not for that."

"I understand," Chloe said softly. Not everyone responded to grief in the same way. "What took you to Benson?"

Her brother's brown eyes were grateful. "No plan without a contingency. Mrs. Pine cannot travel far from the orphanage, so I wanted to approach Dot's new 'family.' If they genuinely were good people, they'd want to pay the penalty to dissolve Dot's contract, and possibly even bring legal proceedings against Miss Spranklin."

"I'm sensing a '*but*,'" Elizabeth murmured.

Graham made a face. "I had to present myself in my guise as a parent of one of the children, so I couldn't tell them Dot was a fugitive and I knew where she was being harbored. In fact, I couldn't even say her name. Any mention of 'that orphan' upsets their 'real' daughter. They sent her away for a reason."

"Poor Dot," Chloe whispered.

Mrs. Pine had believed she was giving the girl the chance of a lifetime, just like Chloe and Tommy. Instead, Dot had been submerged into one untenable situation after another.

"Dot's 'family' is satisfied with their choices," Graham said tightly. "Miss Spranklin's school has a reputation for providing structure and discipline, which is what they feel Dot is missing in her life. They think she should be grateful for this generous opportunity."

"The only thing Dot is missing," Elizabeth ground out, "is someone who loves her."

"No," Chloe said softly. "She has that, no thanks to them."

"I spent the week interviewing parents and guardians," Graham continued. "It's more of the same. Miss Spranklin targets those who care more about status and discipline than their children's happiness."

"That explains why she doesn't allow visitors," Jacob said. "And why the Christmas and summer holidays are so short. It eliminates families who want to see their children. Didn't Dot say most of the girls are left there year-round?"

"It also explains why the musicale is so important," Chloe added. "It gives the parents and guardians a chance to assure themselves they've done the right thing, and that their charges are just fine in Miss Spranklin's care."

Tommy nodded. "It lets them *look* like they care, without actually requiring them to take an active interest in their wards' lives. Especially the girls who were orphaned and fell upon the benevolence of a parish or a distant relative. They're able to pat themselves on the back for having done the 'right' thing."

"*We* will do the right thing," Chloe said fiercely.

It could have been any one of the Wynchester siblings in a contract with someone like Miss Spranklin instead of being adopted by Bean. They'd been loved and given every advantage, not browbeaten and exploited. Miss Spranklin wasn't just stealing the wages from her charges—she was stealing years of their lives. Entire childhoods spent in servitude to a woman who only cared about herself.

"It's worse," Graham said. "The 'employment' she finds for them is at much lower wages than the usual rate. The new owners don't know the lies Miss Spranklin has told, and the girls themselves don't realize how deeply they've been taken advantage of, both at the school and in their new homes. And thanks to the deeply affordable wages, their new employers have no incentive to question their luck."

"They know it's unethical," Chloe said slowly, "but they don't know it's illegal."

"*Is* it illegal?" Tommy asked.

"I suppose the girls 'agree' to their new circumstance," Graham said.

"Girls who cannot read and have no other options," Chloe scoffed.

These were plights Parliament *ought* to pay attention to. Children and the poor. Instead, the House of Lords cared so little that their sessions could meet quorum with only three souls present.

Chloe clenched her teeth. "Teaching girls marketable skills is commendable. Exploiting them until they drop of exhaustion is contemptible. Sending paying parents false reports is unethical *and* illegal." She smiled, triumphant. "It's *fraud.*"

All she needed was proof from Miss Spranklin's office. Once they could prove the letters home were forgeries and that girls Miss Spranklin was contractually obligated to educate were being sent to work with garnished wages instead, the Wynchesters wouldn't just shut down the school.

They could send Miss Spranklin to gaol.

CHAPTER 12

"*R*eady to dance?" Chloe asked.

Tommy's eyes glittered wickedly. "For Bean, I'm ready for anything."

"Marjorie will be here soon." She had gone for reinforcements an hour earlier. "Is everyone else in place?"

"Even the rats are ready," Tommy promised.

Chloe grinned back at her. "Let the game begin."

Throngs of parents, guardians, and hopefuls filled the entryway of the Spranklin Seminary for Girls. Even though the windows were open and the fire unlit in the salon hosting the musicale, the air was already overwarm from so many bodies in one place.

This plan *had* to work. Not just because it was their final opportunity. Construction laborers arrived in the morning, and Miss Spranklin was in the salon signing up new students to fill the additional rooms.

The plan had to work because if it didn't... it would be Chloe's fault. She was the one who had chosen her own family over the plight of these girls. It had only been for a week, but that was little comfort when their lives were hell, either stuck in the scullery of the school where they should be learning, or off indentured to a family without ever seeing a farthing of their wages.

She and Tommy stood at the edge of the chaos, in the empty corridor that led to the wards and Miss Spranklin's private office. Tommy, dressed as dancing-master Mr. Jones, was part of the entertainment.

Miss Spranklin would not step from center stage until the painstakingly orchestrated reel was danced and the last melody was played.

Unfortunately, given that only the elder girls could play anything at all, this did not afford the Wynchesters as much time as they might have liked. Rehearsals had taken less than ninety minutes. Chloe assumed Miss Spranklin would wax poetic between performances, but anything could go wrong, and there was no time to waste.

"If Miss Spranklin attempts to leave the stage, distract her," Chloe told Tommy. "If you cannot stop her for any reason, make the sign and Jacob will take action."

Tommy nodded. "And Graham?"

"He's in place."

"What about the..." Tommy's jaw slackened as she stared at something down the corridor over Chloe's shoulder. Tommy's next words were a breathless whisper. "*Who* is *that?*"

Chloe turned to look.

Tommy grabbed Chloe's arm before she could turn about.

"Don't look," Tommy hissed, "or she'll know we're talking about her."

"*I* don't even know who we're talking about." Chloe tightened her hold on her basket. "Describe, please."

Tommy's gaze softened. "She looks like a literal angel. Golden hair in perfect ringlets... more lace than I've ever seen anyone wear in my life... plump, rosy cheeks..."

"*Tommy.* This is not the time for a tendre. We have orphans to save." Chloe straightened her sister's cravat. "You can talk to the pretty lady later."

"*Talk* to her?" Tommy's words were strangled, and her face went bright red. "I can't *talk* to her. I can barely look at her and think at the same time. Besides, we have orphans to save."

"That's what I just—"

Tommy dashed off, threading through the noisy, milling crowd before Chloe could finish her sentence.

"'Orphans to save' is what *I* just said," Chloe grumbled as she turned down the corridor.

Good God, Tommy was right.

That was a *lot* of lace.

And a problem.

It wasn't just one woman blocking the exact corridor that Chloe needed to sneak down unobserved. It was an entire gaggle of women. Five of them, with the ball of lace in the center.

"They can't see me," Chloe muttered to herself. She was invisible to everyone, especially society ladies. These looked the same age or younger than Chloe herself, and were not accompanied by husbands or children.

Without meeting their eyes, Chloe pasted on a vague expression and began to stroll down the corridor, casually but purposefully. She didn't wish to appear as though she were in a hurry, but nor did she want to give them an opening to strike up a conversation.

She almost made it.

"Good evening!" two of the ladies chirped at once. Their expressions were slightly befuddled. "Do we know each other?"

"No," Chloe said quickly.

"But you look so…" mused another.

The ordinary, "vaguely familiar" features that allowed Chloe to meld with any environment were causing her to stand out amongst this particular crowd of women determined to be friendly at all costs.

Should she keep walking? She should keep walking.

But if she *did*, that would be rude, and rude was memorable.

Blast it all. She was going to have to make small talk.

"Good evening," Chloe responded tightly and tried to inch past them unobtrusively.

"Are you the mother of one of the children?" asked a young lady with dark hair and a pert nose.

"I am not," Chloe answered. "I am the French tutor. Are *you* mothers?"

"Heavens no," said the walking lace explosion with the pretty blond ringlets. "We're a reading circle."

Chloe blinked. "A... reading circle?"

The one with freckles nodded. "Do you like to read?"

"Of course she likes to read," snapped the one in spectacles. "She's a *governess*. What kind of tutor hates books?"

"Why is a reading circle," Chloe asked politely, "at a boarding school children's musicale?"

"Oh, that." Pert Nose smiled beatifically. "We do works of charity when we're not reading Gothic novels and vulgar prose. We came to see if this institution is one that we should be donating to."

"When you're not reading... what?" Chloe asked faintly.

"It's not *all* Gothic novels and vulgarity," said Lace Explosion.

"It's *mostly* Gothic novels and vulgarity," whispered Freckles.

"And then we drink wine and eat cakes!" said Spectacles.

"You should come," chirped Pert Nose. "What was your name again?"

"She didn't give it," said Lace Explosion.

"Well, surely she *has* one," said Spectacles.

They all looked at Chloe expectantly.

She could see that the fastest way to be rid of them was to agree with whatever they said—and, honestly, their reading circle sounded like the greatest idea ever invented—so she forced a quick smile.

"I'm Jane Brown," Chloe said. "Thank you so much for the lovely invitation."

"Do come," said Pert Nose. "We meet at Philippa's house on Thursdays at three and talk for hours. Oh! I'm Gracie, and this is—"

Chloe's stomach tightened. Her bad feeling about this group was worsening.

"Full names, Gracie," Freckles said sternly.

Gracie's cheeks colored. "I'm Miss Grace Kimball. This is Miss Philippa York, in whose well-appointed sitting room we and the other ladies discuss highly inappropriate literature—"

"We also read serious works," Spectacles interrupted. "And plenty of non-fiction."

Freckles rolled her eyes. "Not when it's *my* turn to pick."

"—and this young lady is—" Gracie continued.

Chloe was no longer listening.

Miss Philippa York.

The beautiful, blond-ringletted, literal-angel-on-earth that had caused Tommy to stop in her tracks in the middle of a rescue mission was none other than the generously dowried, highborn young lady angling to marry the Duke of Faircliffe.

The statesman Chloe had watched and listened to and—oh, very well, *ogled*—through a tiny hole in an attic for the past decade.

This was the future Duchess of Faircliffe.

"Yes, of course," Chloe forced herself to say briskly. "What an honor. I'd be delighted to attend the next reading circle." She would do no such thing. "But you should hurry to the salon so that you don't miss any more of the performance. I'll be there in a moment. Please don't wait for me."

"Oh, she's right!" said Gracie. "The music has started."

"*Thursday,*" Spectacles called out over her

shoulder as the ladies bustled down the corridor toward the salon.

Chloe would definitely not be attending any sort of riotous, extremely amusing, weekly literature appreciation event with wine and cakes and friendly, vivacious young ladies... hosted by the type of dazzlingly perfect woman the Duke of Faircliffe *did* pay attention to.

She clenched her teeth and tightened her hold on her basket. She was not jealous. She didn't even *like* the Duke of Faircliffe.

Not anymore.

Over the past weeks of countless returned letters and endless rebuffs in person, Faircliffe had shown his true colors as a lofty, smug, self-centered knave. The only thing Chloe wanted from him now was the rightful return of the Wynchester family heirloom.

If Philippa York thought she could melt that pompous arse's icy heart, then she was welcome to him.

Chloe had orphans to save.

CHAPTER 13

*C*hloe pulled out her pocket watch and grimaced.

Ten minutes.

Those gracious, sociable, vexingly entertaining connoisseurs of depraved literature had managed to waste ten precious minutes of rescue time.

Now that the corridor was empty, Chloe gave up all pretense of nonchalance.

She tightened her hold on her basket and burst into a sprint, skidding around the corner past the wards, past the kitchen...

Here.

Miss Spranklin's private office.

Chloe dropped to her knees to peek through the keyhole. Dim light filled the room from wall sconces.

She fished in her pocket for her iron picks and set to work on the lock.

The first trick was to push up... there, just like that. The delicate part was not letting the lever drop whilst the other pick... jiggled... and teased... and coaxed... until...

In.

She sprang to her feet, flung open the door, and closed it tight behind her.

Miss Spranklin's private office.

The room was small but did not feel cramped. Likely because nothing was out of place. The floor was empty, the surface of her desk was empty, and the bookshelves lining the walls were meticulously organized. There were no paintings or flowers or little personal touches to give an indication of what sort of person spent her time within these walls.

Chloe supposed that in itself *was* an indication.

She peeked through the curtains. The window frames were nailed in place and painted shut. Apparently, Miss Spranklin preferred to swelter in the summertime than risk easy external access to her private office.

Chloe smirked. Unluckily for Miss Spranklin, Wynchesters were not limited to doors and windows. With a stone from her basket, Chloe gave a *tat, rat-a-tat, tat* on the fireplace to let Graham know she'd breached the locked door.

An answering pattern sounded against the brick of the chimney, followed by a soft rustle high above.

From his position on the roof, Graham could not be seen from the windows. He was sequestered behind a gable on the side opposite the road, well out of view of the carriages.

For now.

Chloe looked about the room. She needed to find a ledger or album containing contracts, and there were shelves everywhere. Books squeezed side by side upon each shelf. It would take hours to flip through each volume in search of the one with damning evidence of Miss Spranklin's unconscionable actions.

With a frustrated sigh, Chloe turned to the first bookshelf and checked the spines of its volumes.

Unmarked.

Of course it wouldn't be simple.

She picked up the first book and thumbed the pages, sending up a choking cloud of dust. Shopping lists. Who kept old shopping lists?

Chloe put down the book and picked up another. Rents paid on the current building. That was financial, at least, though it didn't help in the slightest.

She flipped through the next book, and the next, and the next.

Something light fell down the chimney. Another of Chloe's wicker baskets, this one attached to a rope so that Graham could pull the incontrovertible proof up and away the moment Chloe found it.

If she found it.

The girls were half an hour into their performance.

Chloe glanced about in desperation. For such a small office, it contained far too many journals. How did Miss *Spranklin* find the ones she needed?

With a quick intake of breath, Chloe rushed to the escritoire and seated herself in Miss Spranklin's chair. The headmistress would not keep important volumes far from her reach.

But there were no books on the escritoire.

None in the drawers.

The floor surrounding the desk contained a parasol, a pair of boots, and a shawl half-covering up some kind of old wooden...

Strongbox!

She tossed the shawl aside to reveal a rectangular wooden box. This was exactly where Chloe would put something that she didn't want anyone else to stumble across. Well, not *exactly*. Chloe would have chosen an iron strongbox, like the sort used in ships.

And then hidden it beneath a floorboard or behind a false wall.

As she placed the box on the escritoire, coins jangled inside. She inspected the lock. It was trickier than the one on the door. She worked at it for several long minutes without success, then flipped the strongbox on its side. The way in was not through the lock, but rather the joints or the hinges.

All she had to do was loosen the joints just enough to... There!

Several leather volumes thumped onto the desk, followed by loose papers and a prodigious amount of bills and coins. *The stolen wages.* Chloe picked up a book.

The first page bore the name of a student, the date of ingress, the names and direction of her guardians, followed by notations for marks earned as well as a sequence of dates indicating progress reports had been sent home.

This student had left long before Chloe's tenure. The records seemed to be in chronological order, so she riffled through the pages starting from the back. These would be the most recent acquisitions.

Dorothy.

Agnes.

In order to pen fraudulent progress reports to the guardians of the orphans who were not in classes, Miss Spranklin had no choice but to keep a record of the girls' names and original addresses.

The journals also contained the names and directions of the employers she'd sent orphans *to*, in order for Miss Spranklin to ensure she received their monthly wages. In the meantime, she continued to collect school and housing fees from the families and parishes. It was unethical, illegal, and now thoroughly documented.

Miss Spranklin's meticulousness—and greed —would be her undoing.

Chloe picked up the papers. Contracts! She put everything back into the strongbox, the documents, the ledgers, the stolen funds, then carried it over to the fireplace. Carefully, she placed the unlocked strongbox inside of the basket, and gave the rope three quick tugs.

That was Graham's signal. The basket disappeared up the chimney.

She closed the door behind her and hurried back down the corridor toward the sound of the pianoforte.

The music stopped.

Chloe's heart skipped. What if Miss Spranklin had noticed her French tutor's conspicuous absence? Chloe strode faster toward the anteroom. If Miss Spranklin had made it past Tommy, Jacob would launch his distraction. It would happen in three... two... one...

A piercing scream came from the salon.

Shouts of alarm and the confusion of chairs crashing into each other filled the air.

Pale, wild-eyed ladies clutching smelling salts burst from the salon, practically trampling each other in their haste to dash through the entryway and out into the night.

"*Rats!*" came the call from inside the salon. "Miss Spranklin's school is infested with rats!"

That was Elizabeth, who continued the cry in various voices projected from all corners of the salon.

"Rats carry plague!" came another shout, which was almost certainly still Elizabeth.

"Run for our lives!"

After the first wave of stampeding students and guardians came the reading circle ladies Chloe had met in the corridor. Miss Philippa York and her friends looked more confused than panicked, but they were caught up in the flow of running bodies and had no choice but follow the river out of the door and into the street.

Men were fleeing now, too, dragging wives and children with them. They were reacting more from panic than from logic, but to be fair, when Jacob received the signal, he *had* poured six large baskets of rats and three large baskets of mice in through the open windows.

"I will never let a child of mine anywhere near this school again!" came a shrill voice that was no doubt also Elizabeth. "To think my Annie lived in filth!"

"I would never allow *any* child near a hovel run by Miss Spranklin!" answered an indignant gentleman that was also probably Elizabeth.

By now, the panicked, fleeing guests would feel much the same way. Parents and guardians ran with their hands locked with their children and wards. Frocks and tailcoats disappeared into the night.

As the salon and the school emptied of potential customers, Miss Spranklin stumbled out into the entryway and turned dumbfounded eyes on Chloe. "Miss Brown! What on earth is happening?"

"Follow me." Chloe linked her arm through Miss Spranklin's and guided her out through the door and toward the carriages. "Hurry!"

Miss Spranklin had to trot to keep up. "Where are we going?"

"Right here."

The door of a smart carriage swung open and two Bow Street Runners leapt lightly to the ground, one of them holding Miss Spranklin's ledgers in his hand.

"What?" she gasped. "How?"

The carriage behind theirs opened to reveal Marjorie, Graham, and a third Bow Street Runner.

An hour earlier, Marjorie had gone to their headquarters, posing as a distraught mother with a child at Miss Spranklin's school. She had begged the Runners for immediate assistance, claiming her daughter was being held in squalid conditions.

"Rats!" screamed one of the mothers. "Everywhere!"

Two of the Runners took hold of Miss Spranklin's elbows. "You'll come with us, madam."

As the Runners bundled Miss Spranklin off to the magistrate, Tommy emerged from the school's servants' entrance, leading a troupe of bewildered girls to the carriages.

"Agnes!" called Dot. "Over here!"

Dot scrambled from the carriage and the two girls ran to each other's arms.

"How can I ever repay you?" Mrs. Pine asked in relief.

"You can help us talk to the girls who have no guardians to go home with," Chloe replied. "They must be frightened, and we need to let them know tonight everything changes for the better."

The remaining coaches contained a small valise of clothing for each child, all of whom would now possess scholarships to legitimate girls' schools in London, courtesy of the Wynchester orphan fund. Graham would use the guardians' directions from Miss Spranklin's ledger to contact the girls' guardians and inform them of their new address.

The other siblings would visit the graduates employed in undesirable situations and offer them their choice of resuming education or placement at a post with significantly higher wages—as well as return the money Miss Spranklin had taken from them illegally.

Less than an hour later, the last of the carriages pulled away, leaving only the Wynchester family coach behind.

"We did it," Chloe said in joy and relief.

"Of course we did it," said Jacob. "We're *Wynchesters*."

All six siblings touched their fingers to their hearts and raised them to the sky.

CHAPTER 14

*C*hloe poked her head through the usual narrow hole in the attic and glared down through the chandelier at the House of Commons.

The Duke of Faircliffe was not present.

He was at the House of Lords, which had failed to install a convenient ventilation shaft from which a lady might spy upon Parliament.

Mr. York—Philippa's MP father—was down below.

He and Faircliffe had worked together on countless projects and committees over the years. Perhaps that was the reason Faircliffe still occasionally dropped by the House of Commons to exchange a private word with Mr. York.

Or perhaps the reason was Mr. York's daughter.

Faircliffe couldn't offer for her yet. It would be unseemly. He was still in mourning, or at least dressed to resemble it.

He was also still willfully ignoring the Wynchesters.

Chloe ground her teeth.

She was going to get *Puck & Family* back. The painting was *theirs*, had been theirs for nearly two decades, ever since they purchased it from Faircliffe's rackety father.

The new Duke of Faircliffe was every bit as scoundrelly as his sire. He held no sympathy for anyone but himself.

The Wynchesters were grieving, too. They'd lost someone they cared about deeply.

It was a *disgrace* that Bean had died without the comfort of having their family heirloom home where it belonged.

Chloe's vision shimmered.

When she angrily blinked away the offending tears, the room below came back into focus.

Wait. A familiar handsome figure stood in the shadows in the back with a black armband around one arm. Faircliffe *was* here. He had come to watch the debate on the proposed Charities Act, just as Chloe had. And now that the discussion was over... he was leaving!

Quickly, she jerked her head out of the aperture and raced to the stairs, scrambling down the endless wooden steps as fast as her black crape mourning dress allowed.

By the time she burst outside into the drizzly gray afternoon, Faircliffe had almost reached the unmistakable coach-and-four bearing his family crest.

"Your Grace!" she yelled, then gave up on politesse. "*Faircliffe!*"

He paused, and she ran faster, heedless of the mud splattering on her skirts and legs as her boots splashed through muck and puddles.

"Faircliffe!" she called again.

He looked over his shoulder. Looked right through her, as though a screaming, black-clad woman with a tear-streaked face flapping her arms like the world's largest crow was a sight too quotidian to be noticed.

"Fair—" Her voice trailed off. It was too late.

He was already inside of his coach and rolling away. There was no hope of catching up with him.

Chloe stopped to catch her breath, bent over beneath the rain with her hands on her thighs, watching the elegant coach-and-four disappear from sight. Damn him! She swiped the wet hair from her eyes and stalked back toward the shelter of the attic.

The duke had slipped away from her this time, but he could not do so forever. If Faircliffe didn't return their portrait by the time the mourning period was over... he was going to wish that he had.

She'd snatch that painting right out of his grasping hands even if she had to slide down his ducal chimney to do it.

The next time the Duke of Faircliffe crossed paths with Miss Chloe Wynchester...

He would *never* forget it.

ACKNOWLEDGMENTS

As always, I could not have written this book without the invaluable support of my critique partner, beta readers, and editors. Huge thanks go out to Rose Lerner and Erica Monroe. You are the best!

Lastly, I want to thank my *Historical Romance Book Club,* and my fabulous street team. Your enthusiasm makes the romance happen.

Thank you so much!

THE DUKE HEIST

SNEAK PEEK

*To anyone who has ever hoped
for a place to belong*

*And to Roy,
for everything*

CHAPTER 1

March 1817
London, England

Miss Chloe Wynchester burst through the door of her family's sprawling residence in semi-fashionable Islington, followed closely behind by her sister Thomasina. Chloe's pulse raced with excitement. His Arrogance, the Duke of Frosty Disapproval, didn't have a chance.

Unable to keep her exuberance to herself, she yelled out, "I have news about the painting!"

In a more respectable household, a young lady might expect censure for being so vulgar as to shout, even within the confines of one's own home. Such a young lady might also be rebuked for donning trousers and strolling about Westminster under an assumed identity.

Chloe was grateful every single day not to have such limitations.

Her roguish brother Graham appeared at the top of the marble stairs, delight and disbelief writ across his handsome face. He was used to being the one with shocking news to share. "Don't stand about. Come up to the Planning Parlor at once! I'll ring for tea."

Exchanging grins, Chloe and Tommy dashed up the marble stairs, their gray cotton trousers allowing them to take the steps two at a time. In seconds they joined Graham in the Planning Parlor, the communal private sitting room the six siblings used for plotting their stratagems.

Chloe and Tommy tossed their matching beaver hats onto the long walnut-and-burl table in the center of the sound-dampened room.

Tommy rubbed a hand over her short brown hair, causing it to spring up at all angles. Graham moved a pile of scandal sheets from the table to the map case to make room for refreshments. Tommy and Graham launched themselves into their favorite needlepoint armchairs, between two large windows outfitted with heavy calico curtains of ruby and gold.

Chloe was far too excited to sit. Instead, she paced the black slate floor, which still contained traces of chalk from the last planning session. She paused before the unlit fireplace and lifted her chin.

For as long as she could remember, two paintings had always hung above the white marble mantel. One of them had been missing for the last eight months.

But it wouldn't remain missing for much longer.

"The Planning Parlor feels doubly empty without our Puck," Graham said gruffly.

"Not just the Parlor," Tommy corrected. "Our entire house."

Our lives.

No one said the words out loud, but they all knew it to be true. The house had belonged to Baron Vanderbean, but the beloved painting belonged to all of them.

Bean had rescued his motley brood of orphans over the course of a single summer. Six proud, frightened children between the ages of eight and eleven: Chloe, Tommy, Graham, Jacob, Marjorie, and Elizabeth. Life had taught them to be mistrustful and careful. Coming together as a family had been the most pivotal moment in their lives.

Chloe lifted her gaze to the portrait above the left side of the mantel. Bean's fatherly visage bore a grin that crinkled the edges of his bright blue eyes. It was not at all the thing to smile in one's portrait, which was probably why Bean had done so. Chloe was glad he did. His smile always made her feel loved.

A maid entered the room and began arranging

the tea. Chloe tugged her cravat free, so as not to fill it with crumbs.

Tommy wiggled with excitement. "I can't wait to hear your plan, Chloe. Once Puck comes home, it will feel like having a part of Bean back. Like being whole again."

Chloe's heart pounded in agreement. All six of the siblings would do anything in their power to bring *Puck & Family* home where it belonged.

Before they'd found each other, most of the siblings had never had anyone they could rely on or possessions to call their own. They'd learned the hard way not to develop emotional attachments to people or things.

Bean had offered permanence. A place to belong. A home. He told them they were the children he'd always wanted but never had. From the moment each had arrived on the doorstep, they'd felt loved and cherished in a way they had never known. The oil painting was their first purchase as a family. Their first *decision* as a family. For most of them, it was the first time their voices mattered.

The artist's uncommon skill wasn't why they'd chosen the unusual painting. It was the subject. A forest scene, featuring Robin Goodfellow—the mischievous demon-fairy sometimes known in folktales as Puck—and six fellow sprites of all sizes and hues, dancing about a fire with absolute freedom and joy.

It was the visual representation of what they'd found in each other. Happiness. Unconditional love. The ability to be oneself and to be *bigger* than oneself—to be a team, and a family. That was the most magical part of all. That painting was their soul on canvas.

To the Wynchesters, the painting was a family portrait…and their most cherished possession. It belonged to all of them. It *was* all of them.

"Once Puck comes home, we can get rid of that cherub."

All three gazes swung to the fireplace. An angel-shaped vase stood on the mantel, right beneath the faded rectangle where *Puck & Family* should have been.

A blank spot that matched the empty space in their lives where Bean used to be.

Chloe swallowed hard at the injustice. Nineteen years earlier the prior Duke of Faircliffe had sold them the painting to pay one of his many gaming debts. Then, eight months ago, when he suddenly wanted it back, the family refused. Instead of honoring the original transaction, the duke stole the painting and left an ugly vase behind in its stead, as though that could possibly make up for their loss.

Neither they nor the old duke anticipated a

carriage accident interrupting his journey home —or that he'd succumb to his injuries.

When Bean visited the heir to politely request the return of their painting, the newly crowned Duke of Faircliffe refused to see him.

Rebuff Baron Vanderbean! Chloe's blood boiled. But that was hardly the first of the new duke's endless slights and rejections. He'd always been too lofty and self-important to notice anyone of lesser rank, no matter the justification.

Later, when Bean caught smallpox, he refused to allow the children into his sickroom lest he expose them to the disease. They threw themselves into retrieving the painting, and cursed Faircliffe when Bean slowly slipped away, without the safe return of their heirloom . Then or now, the Wynchester family couldn't command a single second of the new duke's time. She ground her teeth.

According to the society papers, the Wynchester children were nothing more than a dead baron's charity orphans—someone you might toss a coin to out of pity but never deign to speak to on purpose.

She didn't care what Faircliffe thought of her. Chloe was *glad* to be a Wynchester. She wouldn't trade a single moment for the boring, buttoned-up life of the beau monde.

Chloe was used to being invisible. It was her greatest talent and often the reason for the success of their clandestine missions. It had begun as a game.

When the six siblings were children, Bean taught them to play Three Impossible Things to give them skills and confidence. They gathered information, breached barriers, and performed feats of daring.

Later, their team became the specialists to turn to when the justice system failed those in need. The Wynchesters snuck food and medicine into prisons, exposed workhouses and orphanages with draconian practices, tracked down libertines who despoiled for sport, rescued women and children from abusers, delivered aid and supplies to those who needed it most. Bean had taught them nothing was impossible. Everyone deserved their best life.

Their missions gave them purpose and adventure. Chloe loved slipping about unseen, doing good works beneath people's noses. But being overlooked on purpose was one thing. Being dismissed out of cruelty was far worse.

"We no longer have to beg," Chloe announced. "We can steal it back from Faircliffe, just as his father did to us."

Graham added another tea cake to his plate. "How will we infiltrate the duke's terraced fortress? That town house is as tightly locked down as His Loftiness himself. Do we even know where he's keeping the painting?"

Chloe grinned at him. "We don't have to. I know where it's going to *be*."

He set down his cake. "Where? How?"

She leaned back. "I sometimes watch parliamentary proceedings from the peephole in the attic—"

"Sometimes?" Graham rolled his eyes. "When have you missed one? And what does your obsession with politics have to do with getting Puck back?"

"Well, if you would let me finish." Chloe pilfered her brother's tea cake and took a bite from the corner, chewing with exaggerated slowness before swallowing. "As I was saying, today Tommy disguised us as journalists and we sneaked into the Strangers' Gallery, where we sat behind Mr. York—"

"Wait," Graham interrupted, his brown eyes gleaming. "Mr. York, the MP whose daughter is rumored to have caught the Duke of Faircliffe's eye?"

"It's more than a rumor," Chloe said sourly. "We overheard Faircliffe say he intends to give *Puck & Family* to Mr. York's daughter Philippa as a courting gift."

Graham's face purpled. "Give away *our* painting? That *knave*. It's not his to give!"

"That's the bad news," Chloe agreed. She affected an innocent expression. "The good news is that my 'Jane Brown' alias has an invitation to Miss York's weekly ladies' reading circle. I met her when I was on that mission at the dreadful school for girls. Philippa was visiting with a charity group and—you know what? It doesn't matter. The important part is, I have access to the home where the painting will *be*. It's our chance!"

Her brother pinned her with his too-perceptive gaze. "You accidentally bumped into the Duke of Faircliffe's future intended and now have a standing invitation into her household? That's a bit of good fortune."

"Er...yes." Chloe became suddenly enthralled by her tea. "A very lucky, completely random coincidence."

It was definitely not because she read the same gossip columns as her brother and wanted to see for herself what kind of woman attracted the Duke of Faircliffe's attention.

Chloe had passed by him any number of times —not that he noticed. He didn't even acknowledge her when she'd placed herself in his direct path to demand the return of her family portrait. Barely a syllable had escaped her lips before he strode right past her toward something or someone he actually cared about.

Blackguard.

"Now that we know when and where to act, we can play the game and get the painting." Chloe counted the Impossible Things on her fingers. "First, ingratiate myself with the reading circle. Achieved. Second, retrieve *Puck & Family* once Faircliffe delivers it. Third, replace it with a forgery so no one suspects a thing. It all happens on Thursday."

Graham frowned. "Why would Faircliffe wish to interrupt a reading circle?"

"He doesn't know he's going to." Chloe smirked. "The Yorks are surprisingly crafty."

"Even a stiff, scowling duke like Faircliffe is a catch worth bragging about," Tommy explained. "Mrs. York will want witnesses."

"*We* don't want witnesses," Graham pointed out. "Wouldn't it be safer to bump into Faircliffe on the street and 'accidentally' swap his rolled canvas for ours?"

"It would indeed," Chloe agreed, "if Faircliffe happened to stroll through Grosvenor Square with a rolled-up canvas. But the painting is framed, and the duke will arrive in a carriage where the York butler will be watching."

Graham lifted his tea. "There aren't a lighter set of fingers in all of London, so I've no doubt you can nick the canvas. And we'll ask Marjorie to create the forgery."

All six Wynchester siblings were talented in

their own ways. Marjorie was an extraordinary painter who could replicate any artwork to match the original.

Chloe smiled. "Marjorie finished ages ago. I just needed an opportunity to exchange canvases. And some way to smuggle it out without anyone noticing."

She swapped Graham's spoon with Tommy's fork as she thought. Coins and keys were easy objects to palm, but a rolled-up canvas was much too big.

"Could you strap a tube to your leg?" Tommy asked.

"Perhaps if I walked very carefully..." Chloe mused, then shook her head. "I would have to lift up my skirts to strap on the tube, and being caught like that would be worse. What I need is—"

"Kittens." Their rugged elder brother Jacob strolled into the Planning Parlor with a lopsided basket in his strong arms. "Most ladies love kittens almost as much as a good book. If you were showing off a new pet..."

Chloe tensed. Although hints of fur clung to Jacob's ripped and patched waistcoat, she'd learned to be wary. The last time her brother had entered a room with a basket, he was trying his hand at snake charming. If she hadn't been wearing her sturdiest boots… "Do you really have a kitten in there?"

"Ferrets," he admitted, his dark brown eyes sparkling. "But I have the perfect solution out in the barn. Tiglet is the best of all the messenger kittens."

"Messenger…kittens?" she echoed faintly.

"Like pigeons, but terrestrial," Jacob explained earnestly. "More fur, less filth. The perfect cover. He can find his way home from anywhere. He'll be a splendid distraction. Because where there's chaos—"

"There's opportunity," Tommy finished, eyes gleaming.

Chloe held up a finger. "First rule of Three Impossible Things: No plan without a contingency."

Graham brightened. "May I suggest—"

"Your acrobatic skills are awe-inspiring, brother, but unnecessary in this instance."

Graham's shoulders caved. "When will it be my turn?"

"Whilst I don't anticipate the need for trick riding on the back of a racing stallion," Chloe assured him, "a *driver* would not be amiss. Just in case I must flee in too much haste to flag down a hackney."

"No hack required." Graham straightened. "We can't risk one of our carriages being recognized, so I'll drive a substitute that cannot be traced to the family."

Tommy cocked her head. "If there is a queue of carriages awaiting their literary-minded mistresses, how will Chloe know which coach is the right one?"

"Mine will have red curtains…and a conspicuously displayed glove for good measure." Graham's eyes lit up. "Better yet, I will not only be the first carriage you come to. I'll be in the coachman's perch. You shan't miss me."

"No plan without a contingency." Jacob's curly black hair dipped as he peeked into the basket of ferrets. "What if the Yorks' staff insist you move the carriage?"

Tommy clapped her hands. "Elizabeth will distract them."

When Elizabeth threw her voice, no one could tell where it was coming from. Their sister could emulate an entire crowd of distractions. She was also handy with a sword stick. Either skill would do the trick.

Graham turned to Chloe, his eyes serious. "If we get separated for any reason, go somewhere safe. I'll find you."

She grinned back at him, exhilarated by the upcoming adventure. *Puck* was finally coming home. "The reading circle will have a wonderful afternoon. Other than a wee interlude with

Tiglet, the most memorable event will be Miss York charming the Duke of Haughtiness."

Graham lifted a broadsheet. "Their alliance will be the talk of the scandal columns. No one will remember anything else. Which is too bad, because I rather enjoy their wild conjecture about us. One of my favorite columns claims: 'Such a large, isolated house could contain dozens of them!'"

Chloe wrinkled her nose. "Those gossips make us sound like *bats*."

"I like bats." Jacob scratched beneath the chin of one of the ferrets. "Bats are fascinating. They have navels like humans and clean themselves like cats. I have thirteen of them out in the barn."

"Please keep them there," Tommy murmured.

"Or give them to His Iciness," Chloe suggested.

"Faircliffe deserves as much." Graham moved the broadsheets in search of his spoon. "No doubt the duke's interest in Philippa York is monetary. Although she has no title, she does possess the largest dowry on the marriage mart. I've been keeping a tally."

"Poor Philippa." Tommy's mouth tightened. "She deserves better."

Chloe agreed. Faircliffe single-handedly lowered the temperature in every room he entered. The man was all sharp cheekbones and cutting remarks. That is, to everyone but her. She was invisible when right in front of him. Even when she was *trying* to be seen.

Graham made a face. "Can you imagine being wed to that block of ice?"

Chloe pushed her teacup away. "I cannot fathom a worse fate."

CHAPTER 2

*L*awrence Gosling, eighth Duke of Faircliffe, was on the verge of achieving what had once seemed impossible: replenishing the dukedom's empty coffers and restoring its tattered reputation.

His father had lived a charmed life on credit he had been unable to repay. And now, with the failure of their country estate's crops, the situation was becoming dire. If Lawrence did not secure a bride with a significant dowry before the end of the season, he would have to send the last of his loyal servants to the streets.

He would not repay them so shabbily.

Lawrence leaned forward in his rented coach and opened the curtain to be able to address his driver. As with all of his father's grievous missteps, each of Lawrence's attempts to restore respect and prosperity had been won at great personal cost.

The sacrifice was worth it.

Lawrence's reputation was spotless, his performance in Parliament impeccable. This season, marriage-minded mamas would have him at the top of their lists. For as long as Lawrence lived, the Gosling name and Faircliffe title would never again be spoken with derision. No heir of *his* would be dismissed, forced to shoulder ridicule and isolation.

Of course, that was because no one realized his shiny reputation hid a very empty pocketbook. The dukedom didn't need *a* dowry. The dukedom needed *the* dowry to end all dowries. A sum so staggering, Lawrence could restore the half-abandoned entailed country estate, repay the last of his father's debts, and have a respectable chunk left over to invest in a stable future.

The dukedom needed Miss Philippa York.

"The terrace house at the corner," Lawrence instructed the driver. "The one with yellow rosebushes."

"As you please, Your Grace."

Using a coach to travel from one end of Grosvenor Square to the other was a shameless display of pretension and excess…and the reason Miss York's parents looked favorably on a courtship between Lawrence and their daughter.

Although he'd sold his last remaining carriage that morning—right down to his prized greys—Lawrence had rented this hack to keep up appearances.

Mr. York was one of the most powerful MPs in the House of Commons. Mrs. York was bosom friends with a patroness of Almack's. They had wealth, status, everything they could ever want—except a title.

After the wedding, the Yorks' daughter would be a duchess, their grandson a future duke. To them, such a jaw-dropping coup would be more than worth any dowry required.

For him it meant a new leaf. The Earl of Southerby was seeking partners for an investment opportunity with very attractive interest rates—*if* Lawrence came up with his portion before the earl quit London at the end of the season. It was not a flashy wager, like the sort his father had made at his gentlemen's clubs, but the steady interest and future profit would provide a strong foundation for years to come.

To Lawrence, marriage to respectable Miss York meant far more than financial stability. His children could be *children*, without fear of mockery or poverty. It would give his sons and daughters the chance—no, the *right*—to be happy.

Everyone deserved as much, including his new bride. Lawrence could not afford to woo Miss

York for an entire season, but he could give her a week or two to get to know him before the betrothal.

He reached for the framed canvas on the seat opposite. "Once the traffic clears, I'll alight at the last house. I shan't be more than half an hour."

But the carriages crowding the Yorks' side of the square did not move. The queue appeared to be idly awaiting passengers. One of the Yorks' neighbors must be hosting a tea. He grimaced.

Lawrence hated tea. He would rather drink water from the Thames.

"Stop here." He reached for the door. "Find your way to the front of the queue so I know where to find you when I return."

The driver nodded and allowed the curtain to fall closed.

Despite residing on opposite sides of Grosvenor Square, this was Lawrence's first call at the York residence. The warm red brick and painted white columns of the impeccable terrace house were bright and clean. Every window glistened in the sunlight, reflecting the azure spring sky or the trim green grass in the square.

Jaw clenched, he strode down the pavement toward their front walk as elegantly as one could with a heavy, brown-paper-wrapped, framed painting clutched beneath one's arm.

Lawrence *could* have brought his last remaining footman along to carry the painting, but he hoped a show of personal effort would add an extra touch of romance to his unusual gift. It was not what he would have picked, but the important thing was giving his future betrothed something *she* liked.

The finality of marriage prickled his skin with equal parts nervousness and excitement. A fortnight from now, when the contract was signed, he and Miss York would be saddled with each other. His palms felt clammy. Was it foolish to hope their union might be a pleasant one? He drew himself taller.

As with all duties, one did as one must.

The door was answered as soon as he touched the knocker. Lawrence presented his card at once.

"Your Grace," said the butler. "Do come in. Shall I ring for someone to take your package?"

"I'll deliver it." Lawrence stepped over the threshold to wait for his hosts.

He and Mr. York had met in the House of Commons and enjoyed spirited debates for most of a decade. Last year, after the premature death of Lawrence's father, he had moved from the House of Commons to the House of Lords. A partnership with Mr. York would ensure vital allies across the two Houses.

All he had to do was remain sparklingly unobjectionable until the banns were read. Once Miss

York married him, her dowry would save the dukedom and secure a better future for his family and his tenants.

The plan *had* to work. It was Lawrence's only shot.

Mrs. York bounded up to him, her hands clasped to her chest as if physically restraining a squeal of excitement. "Your Grace, such a pleasure, I do say!"

The unmistakable sound of female voices trickled from an open door halfway down the corridor straight ahead.

Lawrence's skin went cold. This was supposed to be a *private* meeting. He hated surprises and was inept at impromptu conversations. He excelled in Parliament because he prepared his speeches in advance—just as he had done for today's visit with Miss York and her parents.

Interacting with an unexpected crowd would ensure he made a hash out of his well-rehearsed lines. He stepped no farther.

"Did I mistake the date?" he inquired carefully.

"No, no. Right on time, as always." Mr. York strode up to join his wife. "You're a man who cleaves to duty. A fine trait, I daresay. Very little in common with your father."

"Er...thank you. I should hope I'm nothing like him."

"Quite right, quite right. Your parliamentary

speeches could rival Fox and Pitt. Your father, on the other hand, rarely left his club—or his cups. Indeed, there are many who say—" Mr. York coughed and gave Lawrence a jovial clap on the shoulder. "'Tis no time for gossip, is it, my boy?"

Lawrence affected an affable smile. At least, he hoped that was what his face was doing. He was conscious every day that the Gosling name teetered on the edge of respectability. Mr. York's unfinished intimation had been clear: there were still those who said Faircliffe dukes were a blight on society.

Duke or not, nothing was certain until the contract was signed.

"It is our *honor*, Your Grace," Mrs. York gushed as she fluttered her hands in excitement and impatience. "Is that the special gift for Philippa? Come, you must present it to her at once."

"I admit I can't fathom what beauty she sees in that painting," Mr. York murmured.

Lawrence held the frame a little tighter. Dancing hobgoblins *were* an unusual subject. He did not understand why anyone would want it.

What if, upon second inspection, the young lady realized her error in having expressed admiration for such questionable "art" and laughed in his face when he presented it as a gift? Being able to give an item he already possessed had seemed like serendipity. Now he feared the omen might not be positive. His veins hummed with panic.

"It sounds as though Miss York is entertaining guests." He gripped the frame. "I should return when I'm not interrupting."

"Stuff and nonsense." Mrs. York looped her hand about the crook of Lawrence's elbow and all but dragged him down the corridor. "It's just a few of her bluestocking friends. I'm certain they'll all find it amusing to see what you've brought Philippa."

Yes. Exactly what he was afraid of.

But there was no backing out now. His father's word wasn't worth the breath it floated on, but Lawrence had kept every vow for two and thirty years. Miss York liked the painting; he'd promised to give it to her. On this day. At this time. Nowhere to go but forward.

Besides, "a few bluestockings" was hardly a lion's den...was it?

"Philippa, my dear, look who's arrived!" Mrs. York sang out as they entered a grand parlor.

The room was enormous, with seats for over two dozen guests, and every chair was full.

Lawrence could *feel* the weight of too many gazes landing on him at once.

Half of them, he did not recognize—perhaps those were the "bluestockings"—but the other half were familiar faces from polite society. He swallowed hard. He didn't merely need to impress Miss York and her parents; he needed to charm an entire room.

If only influencing a parlor full of women were as easy as debating customs and excise reform at Westminster with a few hundred of his peers. Quoting the latest committee findings was unlikely to gain him any points here.

He wouldn't acknowledge any of them, Lawrence decided. The situation was too fraught and the chance for error too high. Missteps like smiling at or snubbing the wrong young lady. He would place all of his attention on Miss York. That could be interpreted as romantic, could it not? Here he was with a courting gift, a knight bearing a tapestry of dancing demons for his fair maiden.

Miss York, for her part, was enshrouded in her usual yards of voluminous lace. Only her pink cheeks and dimpled hands protruded from the delicate froth, lending her the appearance of a life-sized doll.

Her eternally blank expression made the resemblance uncanny.

"Miss York," Lawrence began, then paused. He could not kiss her hand with a painting in his arms, and setting it on the ground risked damage. Bowing would be just as unwieldy. He would have to skip the niceties and rush straight to the romance. "I've brought you a humble token of my admiration."

"Ohhh," gasped one of her friends. "What could it be?"

"A painting my mother informed him I might enjoy." Miss York gestured toward a blank spot on the wall. "She intends to put it there."

So. She was not impressed with his courtship gift. Lawrence forced himself to smile anyway.

Miss York didn't smile back.

The rest of the room was alive with whispers.

"Is it a love match?"

"Why else would he wed beneath him? *My* father is a marquess."

"What, did you think he was bringing the gift to you?"

"Do you think she loves him?"

"Who can ever tell what she's thinking? I cannot wait to see the artwork he brought her."

The back of Lawrence's neck flushed with heat.

Yes, Miss York was marrying him for his title. Yes, he needed her dowry. But that didn't have to be all they shared. Even a marriage of convenience could work with a modicum of effort.

But first he had to get rid of this bloody painting.

"Could someone ring for a pair of shears?" he asked politely.

"Here!" Mrs. York trilled.

Two wigged footmen, identical in height and elegant livery, glided into the room and relieved Lawrence of the canvas.

Now was his chance to kiss Miss York's hand. Before he could do so, a maid handed her a sharp pair of metal shears.

Miss York rose to her feet in a rustle of lace.

A wave of whispers once again rushed through the parlor. Lawrence risked a subtle glance over his shoulder.

Every gaze was transfixed on Miss York...except for one. One woman's dark brown eyes arrested him.

She did not seem curious about the gift. Her disconcertingly intense expression was shrewd, as if she could see through the brown paper package, see through his meticulously tailored layers of fashionable apparel, see through *him* to the nervousness and desperation beneath. But she did not look away. Her gaze only sharpened, as if she had stripped him bare and still wanted more.

His throat grew dry. He tried to swallow. An odd prickling sensation traveled up his spine as though the tips of her fingers had brushed against his skin.

He quickly turned back to Miss York. The delivery of the gift had stretched on long enough. If she didn't cut through the paper soon, Lawrence would rip it apart with his bare hands, make his bow, and escape to his waiting carriage before he was forced to follow this performance with tea and small talk.

"If you'd be so kind?" he murmured.

Miss York sliced through the brown paper as though she had little interest in safekeeping the art beneath.

The paper fell away. The painting was exposed. A gasp rippled through the crowd. Whether at the romance of the gesture or because the subject featured a family of mischievous sprites, Lawrence could not say.

"Thank you," Miss York said. "You are most kind."

Was she smitten? Bored? She did not appear to be upset or in any danger of swooning. He gave a gift. She received the gift. *Fin.*

The back of his neck heated anew. He appreciated her extreme lack of drama, Lawrence told himself. After her dowry, her predictability was his favorite trait. A woman like Miss York would never muddy the Faircliffe title with scandal. She was exactly what he needed: no scrapes, no surprises.

Mrs. York burst into loud applause. "Huzzah!"

Everyone in the room followed suit. Everyone, that was, except Miss York and the oddly intense young woman with the mocking half smile.

Her gaze continued to track him, as though she could hear each overloud heartbeat and sense each shallow breath from across the room. He did not like the sensation at all. Despite the roomful of strangers, her regard felt strangely intimate and far too perceptive.

"As soon as the painting is hung," Mrs. York chirped, "we shall all remove to the dining room for a nice, leisurely tea."

Good God, anything but that. Besides his distaste for tea, Lawrence could not court anyone properly while dodging the unsettling gaze of the woman with the pretty brown eyes. Even now, he was thinking of her instead of concentrating on Miss York. It would not do. Once the painting was hung, Lawrence would bolt out the door and into the sanctity of his carriage.

His driver had better be ready to fly.

CHAPTER 3

*C*hloe folded her hands in her lap and did her best not to glare a hole right through the handsome, haughty Duke of Faircliffe.

All of this would have been much easier if Faircliffe would simply *return* the painting. But addressing His Arrogance directly did not work. Chloe and her siblings had pleaded for months, in countless letters sent to his home and dozens of humiliating attempts in person.

His Infuriating Loftiness was far too superior to see reason...or commoners like the Wynchester siblings.

His frigid blue gaze looked right at Chloe—and slid away just as quickly, having glimpsed nothing to attract his interest.

How many times had she and Faircliffe crossed paths? Hyde Park, Berkeley Square, Westminster. Every disdainful glance in her direction was as indifferent as the last. She lifted her chin. Bean had taught her that, to the right person, she would be visible and memorable. Faircliffe was clearly the wrong person.

Not that she *wanted* him to notice her, Chloe reminded herself. The continued success of "Jane Brown" hinged on her uncanny ability to be wholly unremarkable under any circumstances. She gripped the soft muslin of her skirt. Tommy might be an unparalleled genius with disguises, but Chloe needn't do anything at all to blend in and be forgettable.

She possessed one of those faces that was at once familiar yet too ordinary to pick out from a crowd. She was neither tall nor short, ugly nor pretty. Nothing about her stood out.

Her skin wasn't palest alabaster like Philippa York's or golden bronze like her brother Graham's. She was not thin and willowy like Tommy or pleasingly plump like Elizabeth. Her limp brown hair wasn't spun flax like Marjorie's, or blessed with glossy black curls like Jacob's. Chloe was neutral and dull, with nary even a freckle to add a spot of interest.

She was just...*there*, like a dust mote in a shaft of light.

Her perpetual insignificance had helped her

through scrape after scrape. Chloe would never admit how much she wished, just once, to see a flicker of recognition reflected back at her.

Not that her expectations of Faircliffe were high. What type of conceited, coldhearted knave blithely gave away *a painting he did not own* as a courtship gift?

A villain like that could not be trusted or reasoned with. He'd had his chance to deal honorably. Chloe wouldn't beg him for the painting even if she could. At this point, the duplicitous, arrogant blackguard *deserved* to have it whisked out of his hands.

She forced her tense fingers to unclench and folded them in her lap. *Soon.*

"Thank you ever so much for your charming gift," Mrs. York cooed loud enough for the entire party to hear, and likely the neighbors as well. "Philippa is overjoyed."

Philippa did not appear to be overjoyed. Or even middling-level joyful. She bore the same *I am here because I must be* expression she wore at every social function, save the brief occasions when her mother left her side and the reading circle could actually talk about books. Chloe imagined her far more interested in the duke's famed library than in the man himself.

Not that Faircliffe seemed particularly infatuated. A man in love would have dreamed up a gift better suited to his bride.

"My gratitude," Philippa murmured.

The duke looked self-congratulatory. "My pleasure."

Chloe glared at him on behalf of women everywhere who longed for more than token gestures of false affection.

But Faircliffe's kind didn't waste time on matters of the heart. Lords and ladies—or those who aspired to become them—selected their unions with cold practicality. Their minds were muddied not with emotion but with visions of titles and dowries and estates and social connections.

Chloe was *delighted* not to belong to a world like that.

Mrs. York clapped her hands together. "And now…a celebratory tea!"

The duke's face displayed a comical look of alarm. "I don't think—"

"You must join us!" Mrs. York's hands flapped like frightened birds. "The ladies were about to have oatcakes and cucumber sandwiches—"

"We were about to discuss epistolary structure in eighteenth-century French novels," Philippa murmured.

"I never meant to interrupt," Faircliffe said with haste. "I mustn't stay, and in fact—"

"Nonsense! Come, come, all of you." Mrs. York waved her arms about the room, driving her guests into the dining room like a shepherd herding sheep.

Chloe and Faircliffe were both caught in the flow.

Once they passed through the doorway, however, Chloe stepped to one side. She could not take a seat at the table or she would be stuck there for the next hour.

While everyone else was occupied, this was her chance to liberate her beloved Puck. But first, she needed an excuse to disappear. An adorable, furry reason.

She released Tiglet from the large wicker basket. The calico kitten darted between boots and beneath petticoats with a formidable *rawr*.

Mrs. York gave a dramatic shriek in response.

Tiglet scaled several curtains in search of an open window before darting out of the dining room and flying off down the corridor as though his tail were afire.

Chloe gasped as if shocked that her homing kitten was attempting to dash home. "How embarrassing! I'll run and find the naughty little scamp at once. Please don't wait for me."

Philippa glanced up from her place at the table. "I could help—"

"Sit *down*," her mother hissed. "The duke is here."

Philippa sighed. "We could at least ring for a maid or footman—"

"It's really no trouble," Chloe assured her. "Please serve the tea."

With a meaningful glance to Mrs. York, Chloe made several unsubtle tilts of her head toward the Duke of Faircliffe, who was tarrying noticeably, as if reluctant to take his place at the table.

"Oh!" Mrs. York said loudly. "You're absolutely right. Go on, dear. Take your time. Over here, Your Grace. Come and sit by Philippa. We've saved you the best seat."

"Have you met the others?" Philippa gestured at each young lady as she took a chair at the table. "To my left is…"

Chloe slipped from the room at the sound of Mrs. York chastising her daughter for performing introductions out of the order of precedence. Chloe could be gone an hour before anyone would notice.

She wouldn't need but five minutes.

With her basket hanging from her arm, she ducked into the parlor and closed the door behind her. A broken hairpin in the keyhole would not only prevent anyone from entering behind her but would also make it obvious a crime was under way. She would simply work fast.

There was no sense looking for the kitten. Strands of calico fur and unfortunate paw prints on a velvet curtain indicated Tiglet had already found an open window and was well on his way home.

Chloe hurried to lift her family painting from the wall and carried it behind a chinoiserie folding screen in the corner. Cutting the canvas free was not an option. The replacement must look identical to the original, and besides, she would never damage an object that meant this much. Quickly she lay the frame facedown and removed her tools from the basket.

Marjorie had drilled Chloe on mounting and unmounting canvases until her fingers were callused and she could perform the maneuver in her sleep. Up came the grips, off came the backing, out came *Puck & Family*. She rolled it into a scroll the size of her forearm and tucked it into the basket before stretching the forgery over the wooden frame.

This was the tricky part. There was no way to attach the painting without hammering the grips in place. She must do so in silence. If she placed only one grip on each side, and lined each one perfectly with the holes it had come from... There! She hurriedly returned it to the wall.

As long as it stayed there, no one would notice the imperfect craftsmanship. And if one day someone did notice, well, that was none of Chloe's concern. Faircliffe would be the one who had to explain the shoddy frame.

She did not feel sorry for him at all. This was not his painting to give away. For that alone she could never forgive him.

She ran to open the parlor door before anyone noticed it had been shut, and strode past the dining room to the front door without taking her leave from the guests. By now Faircliffe and Philippa were exchanging romantic words, with all of the other ladies hanging on every utterance.

Would anyone realize she had failed to return? Doubtful. If anything, the ladies would assume Jane Brown had slunk off in mortification.

Her throat prickled. She would never know what the other ladies thought of the current novel, but Chloe didn't need reading circles. She was a Wynchester. They had each other, which was more than enough.

Keeping her head down, she headed along the front walk toward the first carriage in the queue. Only when she glimpsed red curtains and a pair of leather gloves on the box did she lift her head toward the driver's perch.

It was empty.

Her lungs caught. Where was Graham?

Distant shouts reached her ears, and her tight

muscles relaxed. Something unexpected must have occurred, and her siblings' planned distraction was in progress.

This was her cue to flee.

Chloe pushed the basket onto the perch, unhooked the carriage from its post, and leapt onto the coachman's seat. Female drivers weren't unheard-of, but all the same, she was glad she never went outside without garbing herself in the plainest, dullest, dowdiest clothes in her wardrobe. No one who glanced her way would bother looking for long.

She set the horses on a swift path out of Mayfair.

Only when Grosvenor Square was no longer visible behind her did she allow herself a small smile of victory.

Their cherished family portrait was coming home. Once she walked in that door with their painting held high—

"Did we escape?" came a low, velvet voice from within the carriage.

Chloe's skin went cold. Who was *that*? Graham wouldn't be hiding in the back of the carriage. A stranger was in the coach! She twisted about and wrenched the privacy curtain to one side.

A handsome face with soft brown hair and

sculpted cheekbones stared back at her, glacial blue eyes wide with surprise.

"*Faircliffe?*" she blurted in disbelief.

"Miss...er...*you?*" he spluttered when he found his voice. "What the devil are you doing driving my carriage?"

∾

THANK YOU FOR READING

Love talking books with fellow readers?

Join the *Historical Romance Book Club* for prizes, books, and live chats with your favorite romance authors:

Facebook.com/groups/HistRomBookClub

And check out the official website for sneak peeks and more:

www.EricaRidley.com/books

ABOUT THE AUTHOR

Erica Ridley is a *New York Times* and *USA Today* best-selling author of witty, feel-good historical romance novels, including the upcoming THE DUKE HEIST, featuring the Wild Wynchesters. Why seduce a duke the normal way, when you can accidentally kidnap one in an elaborately planned heist?

In the *12 Dukes of Christmas* series, enjoy witty, heartwarming Regency romps nestled in a picturesque snow-covered village. After all, nothing heats up a winter night quite like finding oneself in the arms of a duke!

Two popular series, the *Dukes of War* and *Rogues to Riches*, feature roguish peers and dashing war heroes who find love amongst the splendor and madness of Regency England.

When not reading or writing romances, Erica can be found riding camels in Africa, zip-lining through rainforests in Central America, or getting hopelessly lost in the middle of Budapest.

❀

Let's be friends! Find Erica on:
www.EricaRidley.com

Forever

Hachette Book Group

1290 Avenue of the Americas, New York, NY 10104

read-forever.com

twitter.com/readforeverpub

First edition: February 2021

Forever is an imprint of Grand Central Publishing. The Forever name and logo are trademarks of Hachette Book Group, Inc.

The publisher is not responsible for websites (or their content) that are not owned by the publisher.

The Hachette Speakers Bureau provides a wide range of authors for speaking events. To find out more, go to www.hachettespeakersbureau.com or call (866) 376-6591.

ISBNs: 978-1-5387-1952-7 (mass market), 978-1-5387-1950-3 (ebook)

Printed in the United States of America

CW

10 9 8 7 6 5 4 3 2 1

Made in the USA
Columbia, SC
17 February 2021